SUGAR DOM

SUGAR DADDIES #5

CHARITY PARKERSON

--Warning: This book is intended for readers over the age of 18.

Copyright © 2018 Charity Parkerson
Editor: Vicky Reese

Isbn-13: 978-1-946099-37-2
Isbn-10: 1-946099-37-6

INTRODUCTION

***Their off-limits relationship nearly
destroyed them both. So why can't they
let go?***

Detroit crossed a line into the taboo when he fell in
love with his best friend's dad. There'd been a time
when he believed Payne might love him too.
Occasionally, he'd caught glimpses of something in
Payne's eyes. Then, they'd been outed. Now, they're
over, and Detroit isn't the same. He'll never be
the same.

Payne believes in discipline and control. So much so,

he owns a club where people pay lots of money to be punished by him. Detroit is the only person who's ever tested his will. Almost losing his son over the man brought back his strength. No one is worth that loss, except he can't let go. The memory of the way Detroit shook him to his core won't stop haunting him. He doesn't know how to move past it.

Now that Detroit is living and fighting in Vegas, hundreds of miles from Payne, he's trying to start over. That is, until a single moment changes everything.

PROLOGUE

THIS BOOK HAS ALL THE TRIGGERS. ALL OF THEM.

ONE

His twenty-third birthday was almost over. It had passed like any other day. Micah had sent him a card and a bottle of Jack. No doubt his husband had made the purchase. Otherwise, Micah was still months away from twenty-one. Micah had signed the card though. That was nice. Micah felt so damn far away. Everything felt far away since he had more liquor flowing through his veins than blood.

Detroit closed his eyes and savored the suction on his cock. If he didn't look, he could pretend he was somewhere else. With someone else.

"Touch yourself."

Detroit quivered. He'd been waiting for Payne to give him permission for at least an hour. His body ached from the delicious torture. Every muscle jumped as his fingers encircled his cock. He was too aroused. Detroit feared he'd blow at the first tug.

"You're not allowed to come."

A whimper escaped Detroit at Payne's command. He wasn't sure he could obey. Detroit didn't have the same discipline as Payne.

"Please, Payne?" He couldn't stop the plea. His entire body shook with need.

Mismatched eyes, one blue and one green, watched Detroit with heat. He pushed Detroit's hand away. "Your pleasure is mine," he growled, hauling Detroit's hips to the edge of the bed. "Every single one of your orgasms belong to me. Understood?"

"Yes," Detroit cried, clinging to the soaked sheets.

"Try again, Detroit."

Detroit panted. He needed Payne. "Yes, Sir."

"Good boy," Payne said, dipping his head. His tongue swiped Detroit's dick from root to tip before his hot mouth closed around his crown.

Detroit's eyes burned at the memory. He felt sick. His stomach churned. Without thought, he shoved the blonde woman from him. "Get out." Even to him, he sounded dangerous.

She looked worried—like she wasn't sure if Detroit would hurt her.

Detroit flew to his feet, zipping up his pants as he headed for the door. It had been an impulsive move, inviting the woman back to his room from the hotel bar. He held the door open but didn't look her way.

"Are you okay?" she asked as she moved slowly toward the door.

"I just need you to go." Detroit hated himself. Payne had fucking ruined his life. Ruined him from ever enjoying anything. Thankfully, she left without argument. Detroit closed the door and pressed his forehead to the chilled wood. It did nothing to cool his brain. Payne was still there, haunting him. Memories wouldn't stop flooding in.

Payne's thumb traced Detroit's bottom lip. "Happy birthday, gorgeous. What's your birthday wish?"

Detroit wrapped his arms around Payne's neck and shifted closer. While straddling Payne's lap inside the jacuzzi tub, Detroit was the happiest he'd ever been. "I'm getting it right now."

"There has to be more than this," Payne scoffed. "This is your night. Your chance to demand anything."

There was one thing. "Do you remember the first time I showed up at the Den of Payne?"

Payne covered his eyes for a moment and smiled. Detroit's heart turned over in his chest at the sight. "How could I forget? My son's best friend, who I've known since he's sixteen, shows up at my club." Payne shook his head. "I almost tossed you out on your ass."

A chuckle escaped Detroit. "I remember, but I was determined. You have no idea how many bet fights I had to win to come up with the money to ask for what I wanted. Do you remember what I asked for?"

Payne's expression turned heated. "Yes. I also remember what happened afterward."

"Do it again, but this time, do it nude," Detroit begged.

Detroit turned away from the door. His body was on fire in a way only Payne could fix. It had been six of the longest months of his life without Payne. They'd kept their secret for a year and a half, but Detroit had craved Payne's touch for the past four years. There was no one else in his head. Payne took up too much space. There'd been times Detroit had gone elsewhere, trying to burn the man from his mind. Nothing worked. Payne had moved into his head and set up shop, destroying Detroit in the process.

He stripped, trying to cool his overheated skin. No one understood him. Detroit was fucked in the head. Only when someone hurt him did they know the real him. MMA helped, but his sanity was slipping without Payne. He couldn't live like this forever. Nude, Detroit paced the room. He stroked his erection, remembering someone else's hand.

"If you make a sound, I'll stop."

Detroit nodded. He could play this game. Payne's hold tightened painfully. Sweat broke out on Detroit's skin. He doubted his strength in that moment. Only Payne knew how to walk this line between pleasure and punishment.

"You're doing good. I'm proud of you. Do you need more?"

Detroit nodded. He hadn't forgotten he wasn't allowed to speak.

Payne spun him. Detroit's face hit the desk. He heard Payne's belt loosen. Detroit bit his bottom lip. Blood filled his mouth as he fought to stay quiet. The leather caressed his bare ass for half a second before it whistled through the air and bit into his skin. Pre-cum ran down his length. Still, he refused to make a sound.

Payne's wide crown probed his asshole. No lube. That was all the warning Detroit got before his feet left the floor from the power of Payne impaling him.

More blood filled his mouth. His eyes burned and watered. He scratched at the desk, seeking purchase. His body screamed, but Detroit never made a sound.

"You're fucking perfect," Payne whispered against his spine.

Tears filled Detroit's eyes. Payne's praise always moved him. In these moments, he knew Payne loved him, even though he'd never said the words. Detroit needed that love.

Detroit's fist shot out, connecting with the screen of the hotel room's TV. It shattered, spiderwebbing inside its frame. The move tore open his knuckles. Blood bloomed on his skin. It wasn't enough. Not nearly enough. He swiped everything from the dresser—lamp and all. The crashing sound didn't satisfy the rage in his heart. He snatched up what was left of the lamp and swung it like a bat at the French glass doors leading to the balcony. He didn't stop. Glass flew in his face, biting into his skin. He felt nothing. Detroit never felt a thing anymore without Payne. He was broken. Detroit had always been broken. No one else freed him. Now, his vices were lava, living under his skin. His issues were rats, scratching at his brain, making him insane.

Someone beat on the door. He could hear their angry shouts, but nothing stuck. Detroit had moved beyond caring. He caught sight of his reflection in what was left of the glass door. The shattered pieces of his mirrored image struck him to his soul. It was the first time he looked on the outside how he felt on the inside. His throat tightened. The memory of Payne telling him it was over rose to the surface, suffocating him anew.

"I'm sure you would love it if I bent you over this desk right now and lived up to my name." Payne *shoved. The back of Detroit's head hit the closed door. Payne held him there. He dipped his head. At the last second, Payne changed directions and pressed his lips to Detroit's throat. His wide frame felt intimidating rather than safe. Detroit fought the urge to touch him. Run his fingers through the blond curls he loved. "Don't let me ever see you around here again. Because of you, my son hates me."* Payne *released him and turned away.*

Detroit couldn't move. "I'm sorry, Payne. Tell me what I can do." He'd never felt more helpless.

"You've done enough," Payne *said, refusing to look at him. "Micah is all I have, and you knew that. Now, he's god knows where, thinking the worst of me, because I couldn't stay away from you. It won't happen again."*

A piece of broken glass at his feet caught

Detroit's eye. He bent and picked it up. Which piece of him was this? Maybe he should put it back. He stabbed himself in the wrist. Blood shot out in an arc, splashing his chest. Nothing. He felt nothing. Maybe it didn't belong there. Detroit stabbed his other wrist. Same results. Zero fucks. He dropped the glass and stumbled for the bed. Glass cut into his feet. He fell across the mattress and curled into a ball. His gaze stayed locked on the visions inside his head. Everything was slipping away, except the image of Payne. Detroit wanted it all gone. He wanted to fade away until he disappeared. Sleep without waking. He was tired of being different and incurable. Maybe in the next life he'd come back as a monk, seeking peace instead of chaos. Or a tree, mostly unchanging but with a purpose. His vision darkened around the edges. He could hear his heartbeat inside his ears. Each beat came slower than the last. Peace settled over him. Detroit closed his eyes. A sigh of relief fell from his lips. Thank god it was over.

THERE WAS a time when Payne slept soundlessly. Tonight, there wasn't a chance in hell he'd sleep. Temptation crippled him. His hands shook for no discernable reason. He hadn't found the strength to stop holding his phone yet. It was Detroit's birthday. Payne had woken up this morning and the date on the calendar had been his first thought. He hadn't stopped thinking about it since. It didn't matter the clock had passed midnight and technically it wasn't Detroit's birthday any longer. Payne knew wherever Detroit was, he was still awake. Did he think about Payne at all any longer? It had been six months since they'd split. Detroit wasn't the type to keep it in his pants. No doubt the guy had found someone else immediately. Goddamn it. This was hell.

Payne paced and spun his cell phone between his hands. What would happen if he wished him happy birthday? That didn't mean they were together again. In fact, it didn't even mean they were friends. Detroit had spent countless nights at Payne's house and with Payne's son, Micah. The man was like... Payne couldn't finish that thought. If he did, he'd remember he was wrong for ever having touched Detroit. He was, but when he looked back on the year and a half he'd spent with Detroit, Payne didn't feel wrong. All he felt was a deep chasm where Detroit had once been. It was stupid and reckless. For someone like him, those were taboo. His sanity required control. Detroit had let him have control and desire.

Payne froze and stared at nothing. All he saw was Detroit's face. Detroit was beautiful in a way that could stop traffic and draw a crowd. Brown hair and blue eyes with a sexy cleft in his chin, Detroit made people stare. Then, he'd open his mouth, and all his good humor would pour out. Damn. Payne had seen people literally sigh while looking at him. But Payne had seen another side of Detroit too. Dark, needy, and pleading. Payne had to take a breath to control his body's reaction to the memory. Detroit was a sickness living in Payne's gut. The man had almost cost Payne his son. Micah had said several times now he didn't care if Payne and Detroit wanted to be together. Two things stopped him— Micah's expression when he'd realized they were sleeping together and the way Payne had ended things. The thought of ever hurting his son was like a knife in his throat. Every time he remembered the way he'd treated Detroit afterward, he hated himself a little more. Sometimes, there was no right answer— only how he felt.

The sensation of warm lips moving from his throat to his chest in a line of open-mouthed kisses pulled Payne from his dreams. His fingers found

Detroit's hair. If he was fully awake and had his wits about him, he'd take control. Instead, a fuzzy haze coated his mind. He was lethargic and at Detroit's mercy. That didn't stop his dick from going hard.

Payne gently cupped the back of Detroit's head as he kissed his way to Payne's cock. His eyes refused to open. Detroit's hot mouth suckled him. Payne's hips left the bed, seeking more. Detroit was too gentle, yet Payne couldn't find the strength to take charge. He was ridiculously content. Payne stroked Detroit's cheek, enjoying the way Detroit felt beneath his fingertips. There was a pressure sitting on Payne's chest, making it hard for him to breathe. Damn. He cared about Detroit. Too much. Payne had never wanted to make anyone happy like he did Detroit. He urged Detroit higher. Payne needed the man's kiss more than he needed a blow job. There was pleasure and then there was ecstasy. Sometimes they weren't the same.

Payne's phone rang, startling him from the memory. For a split second, hope rendered him useless. He fully expected Detroit's name to appear on his screen. They felt that connected in his mind. Instead, it was Micah. Payne glanced at the clock. It was two in the morning. No good phone calls came at this time. Payne rushed to answer. Fear choked him.

"Hello?"

"Dad." Payne's heart stopped at Micah's tone. "It's Detroit."

"Tell me."

Micah took a breath. It sounded ragged. "Zander called. He says Detroit is in intensive care at Valley Medical. Wyld is having a plane chartered and we're heading out tonight. I thought maybe you'd like to come too."

"Tell me what happened." Micah was purposely not saying. Payne knew his son too well.

"He tried to kill himself."

The blow landed. Payne couldn't draw a single breath. He swallowed. Still, nothing.

"Dad?"

Payne inhaled. Finally, air inflated his lungs. "Yeah. Give me ten and I'll be there."

"Okay. I'm not sure they'll let us see him, but I have to go, you know?"

Payne nodded even though Micah couldn't see him. Micah was Detroit's best friend. Maybe Payne had messed that up, but Micah wasn't the type to turn his back on anyone in their time of need. Payne wasn't the same. There were lots of people he could turn away from. Detroit wasn't on that list. Payne had to be there. If Detroit died before Payne could make things right... he didn't know. Maybe he wouldn't survive it.

"I'll be there soon." That's all Payne could do for now. He prayed he wasn't too late.

TWO

IF PAYNE HAD BEEN ABOARD THE PRIVATE LUXURY jet for any other reason, he might've been impressed. He'd never flown while seated on a couch and feet from a full bar. Micah and Wyld sat huddled together on the loveseat. Wyld kept placing light kisses on Micah's temple while Micah nervously toyed with his husband's fingers. Payne was only mildly curious what Wyld kept whispering against the shell of Micah's ear. He hoped it was words of comfort. Micah looked a mess. Payne had no comfort to give. He couldn't take the silence.

"Tell me what you know."

Micah's gaze collided with his. Payne could see the panic swirling inside his son. They needed to talk. Turning inside themselves was dangerous.

"Um." Micah cleared his throat. "Detroit has been staying at the Luna in Vegas while fighting for one of Zander's companies. He had a match and won. Zander was in town for it. Right before midnight, a call came in to the front desk, complaining about the noise coming from Detroit's room. They said it sounded like he was smashing furniture. Since Detroit is a guest of Zander's, they called him. No one wanted to be the person who upset one of Zander's personal guests, I suppose." Micah took another deep breath. He blinked and visibly swallowed.

Payne's chest tightened.

Micah swallowed again. "Zander says he used his personal code to get inside the room when Detroit didn't answer. He found h—" Micah's voice broke off.

Wyld took over. "Zander called the paramedics. He worried there might be some legal ramifications for Detroit over a suicide attempt, so he told them Detroit cut his arms while smashing out the windows. Since he's the owner, he obviously won't be pressing charges for the property destruction. I tried to pay for the damages, but he wouldn't let me."

"Are they sure it wasn't just an accident while he was smashing out windows?"

A tear rolled down Micah's cheek. His chest expanded on a deep breath. "Zander says it was very obvious he'd slit his wrists and laid down to die." Micah's voice gave out on the final word.

Payne's throat swelled. He looked away. The guilt, it was real. He'd known Detroit had issues. But, like an idiot, Payne had fallen in love with Detroit and forgotten to check his emotions at the door. Then they were over, keeping his distance and the door closed to Detroit had taken precedence over any problems he knew Detroit suffered.

He wanted to keep the conversation moving. Keep his son's mind busy and be the adult. His tongue wouldn't work. Time passed in a blur of unreality. Payne couldn't recall a time he'd felt more disconnected from the events taking place around him. He moved when it seemed he should, walking off the plane and to the waiting SUV. Bright lights flashed by as they passed. Payne didn't see a thing. The hospital doors came into view. Wyld led. Payne followed. When Wyld and Micah sat, he did too. They could've been there five minutes or five hours. Payne couldn't tell the difference. It wasn't until he heard Micah speak that he realized Zander was there. Payne didn't bother with the man.

A nurse in blue scrubs came out looking for the

family of Detroit Amherst. Her words were the first to penetrate his fogged brain. "Does Mr. Amherst have any family present?"

Zander motioned toward Micah. "This is Detroit's brother," he lied without flinching.

The nurse focused on Micah. "Mr. Amherst isn't conscious to give his information. Do you mind helping us?"

Micah didn't hesitate. "Of course. I'll do what I can."

She nodded. "He didn't have an insurance card on him."

Micah cut her off. "His job doesn't offer insurance. You can send the bill to me. I'll take care of it."

Payne's gaze swung Wyld's way. He expected Wyld to scoff. Instead, the man nodded along as he rubbed Micah's back. Payne's respect for the man who'd married his son skyrocketed. He didn't have the kind of money Wyld did, but Payne would find a way to repay them. He could take out a loan against his club if the bills were too steep.

"When can Micah see him?" Wyld asked, interrupting the nurse who was obviously only concerned about payment.

She shook her head. "That's a question for the doctor."

Payne bit back a growl and turned away. No one was telling them anything. He was ready to start kicking in doors to find Detroit for himself.

"Here he is now. This is Dr. Hollister. He can help you."

Payne shot to his feet.

The doctor looked too young. His blond hair, green eyes, and hard body belonged on a college student. Not someone caring for an ICU patient. Payne barely stopped himself from demanding a real doctor. The only thing stopping him was the hope of finally finding something out.

The nurse motioned Micah's way. "This is Mr. Amherst's brother."

Dr. Hollister's gaze landed on Micah and didn't budge. It was as if everyone else disappeared. That happened a lot when Micah was around. This was one of those times it worked in Payne's favor. No one noticed when he lingered behind Micah and openly listened to every word.

The doctor took Micah's hand. Rather than shaking it, as Micah obviously intended, the man held on, patting it as he spoke. Payne rolled his eyes.

The man was one of those handsy doctors who thought they were comforting.

"Detroit lost a lot of blood. If he'd gotten here even five minutes later, it would've been too late. The good news is, he's stable. He severed part of his flexor muscle in one arm as well as some nerves. In the other arm, he severed the ligament and nerves. We've repaired what we can."

The doctor kept talking. Payne sat. His head spun. What had Detroit done? It sounded like he'd tried chopping off his hands. Payne's hands shook. He clasped them in his lap. A hand covered his. Payne stared at the man's black wedding band. His brain didn't want to slow and allow him time to catch up. When he finally managed to turn his head, he was more than a little surprised to find Wyld was the one trying to comfort him. Micah was nowhere to be seen.

"Where's Micah?"

Wyld chewed his thumb nail and didn't look Payne's way. "The doctor took Micah back to see Detroit. Since he's in ICU only family can visit."

Damn. Payne wished he'd lied and claimed he was Detroit's dad. His lips wouldn't shape those words. "I'm surprised they're letting anyone see him."

Wyld nodded but still didn't look his way. "Zander says unless Detroit admits to a suicide attempt, the hospital can't prove it."

Payne's knee bounced. The nervous motion was out of his control. He wanted to see Detroit, but they wouldn't let him. He felt useless and angry. Not to mention, sick and guilty. "Maybe I should gather his things from the hotel?"

Wyld finally looked over. There were dark circles under the man's eyes. Payne's chest tightened. He never stopped being struck anew by how much this man loved his son. Payne got tired of always being wrong. "If you feel like you need to be doing something, I'll call you a car. I'm sure Zander will let you in."

Payne nodded and stood. He needed to move. Sitting around wasn't helping. He needed to be useful. God knew he'd failed Detroit in every other way.

NO. That was all Detroit could think. Just no. He stared at the particle board ceiling and let the truth wash over him. Somehow, he was alive. His eyes burned with unshed tears. He didn't want this.

"Hey, sweetie."

Detroit turned his head. An exhausted looking Micah sat at his side. His blond curls stood in every direction as if he rolled from bed and then spent hours running his fingers through his hair. He still looked amazing.

"Always knew you were really an angel." Even to Detroit's ears he sounded hoarse.

Micah's smile was tinted with sadness. "Do you need some water? It sounds like your throat hurts."

"You should go home to your husband."

"My husband isn't at home," Micah said, coming to his feet. He checked the thermos before carrying it to the bed. "Wyld is in the waiting room with Dad." He flashed Detroit a bright smile. "Hopefully, they're not trying to kill each other. Is it okay if I adjust the bed?"

Detroit nodded, and Micah moved him into a sitting position. All Detroit could think was Payne was here. Under the same roof. Micah held the cup while Detroit sipped from the straw. He drank until Micah seemed satisfied since his arms felt too heavy to push the cup away. "Wyld would probably win on crazy factor alone," Detroit said as Micah set the water aside. "Everyone knows crazy trumps strength." And Payne would never hurt Wyld because that would hurt Micah.

Micah hovered like a worried hen while obviously trying to hide his concern. "Nah. Wyld is a lover not a fighter."

"You should ask me everything you want to know before you're forced to intervene between the two." As much as Detroit hated to be the one to acknowledge the elephant in the room. He felt too horrible to dance around the topic. Sleep already wanted to pull him back under.

Micah looked away. "The hospital thinks I'm your brother. You might want to play along if you don't want me kicked out."

"Come on, Micah."

"I'm also paying your bill, so you don't have to worry over that. And Zander won't be pressing charges for the damages to his hotel suite."

"Stop it, Micah." Even to his ears, Detroit sounded tired. "I know you don't like conflict, but please stop."

To his horror, Micah's chest expanded on a huge breath. It sounded ragged as the first tears fell. He'd seen Micah suffer through a lot, but he'd never seen him cry. If Micah had screamed and cursed his name, Detroit could've handled that. Tears were another story. "Everything I read online said not to question you or make you feel guilty." Every word came out sounding broken and Detroit wasn't lucid enough to handle it.

He tried dealing with what he could. "You read something online?"

"Well, yeah," Micah said, swiping at his cheeks. "Zander convinced the police you'd injured yourself by accident so what else am I supposed to do? The hospital is treating you like an accident victim, so you won't be getting the help you obviously need, and I don't know how to help you."

Detroit closed his eyes. He was just so fucking tired. "Don't cry for me, Micah." Each word came out slurred for some reason. "I'll do whatever you want when I wake up. Just don't cry, okay?" He couldn't stay awake, but Micah's tears still hurt his chest. He couldn't make Micah cry. That was cruel.

"Go to sleep, babe," Micah said rubbing Detroit's upper arms and chest. "I'll take care of you."

Detroit drifted off believing every word. Micah was the best at taking care of people.

"HOLY SHIT." Payne couldn't have held back his

reaction if he'd tried. The destruction he encountered as the hotel room door swung open was epic. There was blood everywhere. Payne couldn't stop staring at the bed. Blood seemed to soak every inch. If he hadn't already been to the hospital, Payne would've sworn there was no way Detroit survived. A trail of blood led from what was left of the glass doors to the bed. Payne picked his way through while trying to keep his gaze averted from the mattress. He felt sick. A cold sweat coated his skin. His eyes and nose burned. Payne kept his mind firmly locked on his task.

He opened the closet and found Detroit's luggage. Payne carefully folded Detroit's clothes, showing his love the only way he was allowed. He swept through the room twice, making sure he didn't miss anything. Even if Detroit refused to go home to California with them, he couldn't stay in this room. In truth, if not for Zander, this hotel would never have him back.

With Detroit's bags packed, Payne headed for the door. Without permission from his brain, his gaze slid back toward the bed one last time. Payne wanted to rage and plead with the universe, asking why Detroit would do this thing. But Payne already knew why. He was the only one who saw Detroit and understood, and still, he'd done his part to destroy him even more.

Payne shouldn't have come. He didn't deserve to be at Detroit's side. If he had any mercy in his heart, he'd go back home now, and leave Detroit in peace. Maybe he'd do just that.

THIS TIME the pain woke him. Detroit's arms throbbed in time with his heartbeat. A groan escaped him without his permission.

"Do you need something for the pain?"

Micah was here. That part hadn't been a dream. "Yeah." Damn, his voice still sounded awful. Micah didn't hesitate to push the button to call for the nurse and ask for meds. With that out of the way, he gently rearranged the pillows surrounding Detroit, ensuring his arms were propped up. The pain immediately lessened. Micah was a gift straight from God. Detroit tried forcing his thoughts to stop racing. It was hard to focus on any one thing while hurting. His gaze moved around the room. He spotted his luggage stacked in the corner. "Looks like you've been busy. Did the hotel kick me out?" They'd be stupid not to, but that was fast.

Micah hovered over him, looking worried. At the question, he cast a glance toward Detroit's belongings. "Dad picked everything up for you, so don't worry. You know how thorough he is. Zander said you can come back to the Luna when I decide you're ready. Until then, you'll be going home with me when the hospital releases you."

Great. He'd been reduced to being a child again. Even with that aggravating piece of knowledge, Detroit couldn't move past Payne gathering his things. Had Payne been in to see him while he slept? Fuck, Detroit hated that he cared.

"I don't want to see him." The admission was out there before Detroit knew it would happen.

Micah's gaze moved from watching the door to meet his stare. "Who? Zander? He's not mad at you. He just wants you to get the help you need before coming back to fight. Plus, your arms need time to heal." Micah's features hardened. "And you've lost your goddamn mind if you think I'm letting you stay here in Vegas, as if nothing happened."

Detroit shook his head. "I'm not talking about that. I know I fucked up, so I'll do whatever makes you happy. It's Payne I don't want to see."

Micah's features transformed, closing off his thoughts. "Oh. That's okay. You don't have to worry about Dad. He decided it would be best if he went home. He worried he might do more harm than good if he hung around."

The rock sitting in his stomach was so goddamn heavy. When it came to Payne, Detroit never stopped feeling torn in two. He'd just said he didn't want to see Payne, yet it fucking killed him that Payne didn't want to see him. Detroit didn't know how to stop loving Payne. It seemed like time and distance should've helped. Nothing lessened the pain and soul crushing loss. Thankfully, the nurse arrived, saving Detroit from having to find something to say. Nature took over, transforming Detroit into the fake flirt he'd been his whole life. He pasted on a smile he didn't feel, charming his way through a dose of pain meds. No one would ever understand how relieved he was when they knocked him out, taking him away from the unhappiness that was always there, choking the life from him.

THREE

Dr. Hollister looked too young to be practicing medicine. Not that Detroit cared. He was there because he'd wanted to die. That made it a little hard to balk at the level of care he received. Still, the guy spent entirely too much time mooning over Micah while Micah sat there oblivious.

"Looks like you're going home today. Are you ready?"

Without giving Detroit time to answer the doctor, Micah chimed in. "He's going home with me for a while, so he'll be okay."

Dr. Hollister's gaze swung Micah's way and didn't budge. Detroit bit back a sigh. It had been that way for the past week. The man was obviously intrigued. "I wager he'll be more than okay in your capable hands. And where is home exactly? You know, so I can suggest a good follow-up physician."

"With me," Wyld said, cutting in and making Detroit smile.

The overly confident doctor's mouth lifted in one corner in a wicked looking smirk. "I see." He finally met Detroit's gaze again. "I'd also suggest you find a decent therapist."

Detroit didn't take the bait. He knew the man wasn't an idiot, but that didn't mean he intended to admit to a damn thing. "What time did you say I'm getting out of here?"

"As soon as the paperwork is signed, and all your questions have been answered."

"So, yesterday?" Detroit couldn't stop being a smartass and he didn't know why. He was just cranky as fuck and tired of not sleeping. He wanted out.

Thankfully, Micah had his back. "Detroit fights for the Luna. How long will it be before he can get back to training and working?"

"He can start back immediately on anything that doesn't stress his arms. I'd say he could start on light arm work in about four weeks, and—hopefully—be back to fighting in eight. What sort of work do you do, Micah? I mean, I see here you're the one who's listed as being financially responsible. There are programs if you need help with the bill. We could talk about it later."

"His job is being married to me," Wyld said, sounding bored. "Not only can I afford the bill, I can also afford to have you killed and no one would bat an eye."

Micah switched his gaze between them, looking torn between confusion and horrified.

Suddenly, Detroit was enjoying himself in a way he hadn't in months. "That paperwork would be nice," Detroit said, pulling the doctor's attention his way.

"Sure. I'll call for transport."

As much as Detroit wanted to argue he didn't need a wheelchair out of this joint, he understood it was policy. He gave the man a short nod, and after one last lingering look Micah's way, the man finally left them in peace.

"What the hell?" Micah said, sounding completely lost the second they were alone.

"You might not want to leave this room alone," Detroit said with a laugh.

"Ballsy cunt, isn't he?" Wyld chimed in, eyeing the door like it was at fault for allowing the doctor anywhere near Micah.

"What did I miss?"

Detroit shook his head at Micah's question. As much as he wanted to call Micah a blind fool, he'd learned Micah really wasn't. He was just too damn kind to understand that other people weren't nice unless they wanted something.

Wyld took Micah's hand and brought it to his mouth. "You're too sexy for the doctor to withstand. I think you addled his brain."

Micah blushed. "He was just being nice."

"Detroit is the expert on flirting. Let's ask him."

At Wyld's claim, both men looked his way, expectant. Detroit's throat swelled out of the blue. It was one of those moments where he suddenly felt normal, but normal fit like a cheap suit. He swallowed it down, trying to hide the black wave. "You struck him dumb, sweetie. Even under the threat of death from Wyld, he didn't truly want to give up hope."

Micah shook his head. "You're both crazy. People don't look at me like that. Besides, I'm happily married."

"So?" Wyld said at the same time as Detroit.

Thankfully, Wyld chose to field this one. "Angel, if you'd been married when we met, I don't think that would've stopped me. You make men a

33

little mad with your gorgeous body and sweet demeanor."

"Huh," Micah said, sounding indifferent. "Well, you learn something new every day. I guess it's a good thing I hadn't settled before we met." The way Micah beamed loosened the tightness in Detroit's chest. Micah was happy. That was everything Detroit had ever wanted for him. There'd been times Detroit had worried Micah wouldn't find anyone good enough for him. Someone who also understood him the way he deserved. He'd worried that going home with Micah and Wyld would be a nightmare. That being forced to endure their choking happiness would be the final nail in his coffin. Now, he realized they were exactly the normal and healthy relationship he needed to drench himself in. Hopefully, by the time he was ready to return to Vegas, he'd have a better grip on his future. It couldn't hurt to try. After all, dying hadn't worked out for him.

DETROIT WAS BACK IN CALIFORNIA. Payne could get in his truck and be under the same roof as the man in under twenty minutes. It was hell.

Temptation whispered Detroit's name every second of the day. So many things stopped him from visiting Detroit. The biggest one was the horrible suspicion he was the cause of Detroit's grief. There was also Micah. Payne's son had taken Detroit in. The only thing surprising about that was how Wyld had let Detroit come into his home without the slightest hint of disapproval. Now, that was a man who continually surprised Payne. Probably he should get around to apologizing to Wyld someday for the way he'd reacted to Wyld marrying his son. Payne wasn't good at being sorry. Yet, it seemed as if lately he had more regrets than anything else. Maybe he'd swing by Micah's later today. If he saw Detroit too while he was there, then so be it.

Payne had a two o'clock client he needed to deal with first. He could already feel his personality changing. When he stepped onto the playroom floor, Payne was someone else. This wasn't about sex. Most times, people just needed to be set free. His normal clients tended to be powerful businessmen. People who were used to being in control. Everyone needed something they kept only for themselves. Sometimes, Payne was that something. He was the secret life. The clandestine shameful fetish. He brought people to their knees—literally. Giving them peace satisfied him.

A chiming noise yanked Payne from the mental place he'd gone, preparing for the day. His gaze landed on his phone. Micah's name stared up at him. He shook off the thoughts he couldn't share with his son and answered.

"Hello?"

"Hey Dad. How's it going?"

Payne's lips automatically shaped a smile at the sound of Micah's voice. "Good. I was just thinking about you. Would it be okay if I stopped by later?"

A long silence followed his question. Payne spent a moment wondering if their call had dropped or if Micah didn't want to see him. Finally, Micah spoke, letting him know at least one of those wasn't true. "Um. Would you like to go to dinner instead?"

"That's fine. Will Wyld be joining us?"

"Probably. Is that okay?"

The unsure note to Micah's voice let Payne know it was well past time he apologized. "Of course, but listen, is it okay if I pick you two up? I'd like to speak with you both before we're sitting in public."

Another bout of silence met his question. Payne couldn't figure out if Micah's attention was split or if something else was happening. "Well, maybe we could pick you up instead."

An uncomfortable sounding laugh escaped Payne. "Am I no longer welcome at *chateau de le Wyld?*"

Micah laughed as Payne hoped he would. "It's not that. Detroit is here. He doesn't want to see you." Micah said the words fast—like he was breaking up with a crazed ex and hoping he wouldn't get stabbed.

"Oh." Seriously. That's all he had.

"I'm sorry," Micah said, as if he had anything to apologize for. "He's still healing and just started counselling."

"You don't have to—"

Micah kept talking over him. "He didn't explain why he doesn't want to see you, only that he doesn't. I think it might do him good to talk to you, but it's not up to me what's best for him, you know? So, I'm sorry."

"Stop apologizing," Payne said with a sigh. "Detroit's a grown man. He knows best what he needs. I just hoped to talk to Wyld because I think it's well past the point I should tell him how sorry I am for the way I acted when I learned of your marriage."

"Oh," Micah said, obviously brought up short. "I

mean, you can say all that if you want to, but Wyld knows you're over it. He's not the type to hold a grudge."

"Okay, then. You can pick me up at seven."

"Great," Micah said, sounding relieved.

Payne kept up his end of the conversation until goodbyes were exchanged. It wasn't until after he'd set his cell phone aside that he allowed the hurt to wash over him. Detroit didn't want to see him. It seemed his guilt was well earned. Hearing those words had been all the confirmation Payne needed. He'd played his part in crushing a wonderful man who'd already endured the unspeakable before meeting Payne. Payne tried clearing his mind, getting back into his role. He tried not to take his issues out on clients. Today, he didn't know if he could shove his emotions into a box and seal them away. He leaned back in his seat and stared at the ceiling. The months fell away.

"Micah's in the other room. He'll be up any minute."

Detroit nodded. "I know, but he's expecting me to be here today. When we tried delivering meals for the mission yesterday, there were a few people we couldn't find. I told him I would go back out with him today."

He knew Detroit only went out with Micah to watch his back, but sometimes Detroit sounded like he enjoyed helping the homeless too. "Ah. That explains all the boxed-up food in my fridge."

"I also had news," Detroit said, sounding nervous.

A smile pulled at Payne's lips. Detroit was always so confident. In the moments when he let his guard down, Payne saw a side of him no one else did. It was sexy and endearing. He always made Payne want to touch him. Detroit moved closer. Payne did too. Without thought, Payne's hand lifted. The back of his knuckles brushed Detroit's jaw. He was so fucking beautiful. How was Payne supposed to resist?

"You're here."

Detroit jumped at Micah's overly loud interruption. Payne turned away. He knew if anyone looked at him, really looked, they'd see his heart in his eyes. He was certain anyone with a half a brain would know he loved Detroit. Goddamn it. He didn't know how to stop, but he had a bad feeling he hadn't been quick enough to hide it this time.

Payne flew to his feet and flipped his desk. The anger burst from him in an uncontrollable fit of rage. It was over as quickly as it began. He stared at the mess scattering his office floor and felt... nothing.

Maybe that was the long and the short of it. Without Detroit, he was nothing.

DETROIT STARED at the ceiling as he lifted weights. It was nothing like the amount he was accustomed to, yet it was a struggle. He hadn't expected any of this. There'd been no plan in mind for the future. He sure as shit hadn't realized he'd be starting back over with his workout routine. Thankfully, Wyld had his own gym, saving Detroit's pride. He fucking hated the thought of anyone seeing him like this.

"What would you like for dinner?"

He stood corrected. There was one person who seemed to take perverse pleasure in seeing him at his lowest—Wyld's personal assistant, Cortland. When he'd allowed Micah to bring him home, it hadn't occurred to him that anyone would be living with Micah other than Wyld. He sure as shit hadn't expected to see the haughty asshole who'd told him he could go fuck himself once upon a time at their one and only meeting. All Detroit had been doing at the time was hunting for Micah. First impressions weren't the best between them. The only thing that saved Detroit from raging at the man was the fact that he worked for Micah. Therefore, as Micah's guest, the man worked for him. So far, he hadn't gloated too much.

"I'm cool with whatever everyone else is having."

"It's just us, so..."

That gave Detroit pause. He sat up and wiped the sweat from his face. "Where'd we lose Micah and Wyld to?"

"They've gone to dinner with Micah's father."

Cortland hadn't even said Payne's name. The impact was the same. It was as if he'd walked in the room. The longing hit like a sledgehammer. He had to get out. It was like a million eyes were watching him, judging him, and finding him lacking.

"I think I'll go out too. Do you mind giving me a lift to pick up my car from storage? It's at Haulin' It Storage on Monroe."

"Not at all. That will give me an excuse to check on the progress of one of our tiny home recipients."

Detroit came to his feet. A chuckle escaped him. "You've been spending too much time with Micah, I see. He rubs off on everyone."

Cortland followed him from the room. "I suppose, if you choose to see it that way, then yes. In truth, he reawakened a past dream of mine to help people less fortunate. I used to be one of them, before Wyld saved me, and I always meant to find a way to deserve that blessing."

Cortland's confession drew Detroit up short. He had a hard time seeing the tall, lanky, and perfectly pressed man as homeless. "You used to live in the streets?"

Cortland nodded. "For six years. My parents kicked me out at seventeen when I came out."

For the first time, Detroit felt a hint of connection with Cortland. He sucked in a hiss. "My parents at least let me wait to move until I had a high school diploma and a job. But they let it be known every day, I was no longer part of their family. I don't miss them, but I miss the idea of them." Detroit had no idea why he'd admitted such a thing to someone he barely knew. He shook it off. "Just let me grab a quick shower and I'll be ready to go."

Cortland nodded. "I'll be here when you're ready."

With a nod, Detroit rushed to the bedroom he'd been assigned. It was nicer than any apartment, house, or hotel room he'd ever lived in. Micah seemed to adjust to living in so much luxury without blinking an eye. Detroit spent every second hoping he didn't get anything dirty. Not that it mattered if he did. His bed was always made even though he hadn't touched it. The bathroom was always clean and straight no matter the mess he'd left behind. His clothes were always washed and put away. Detroit never saw anyone cleaning, but it happened. He couldn't fathom having that much money.

The few weeks he'd been here had forced him into one realization for certain—Wyld was a good man. Detroit owed Micah and Wyld everything, but they never made him feel beholden. Every lecture Detroit had given Micah about how stupid he was for trusting Wyld piled on his ever-growing guilt. Micah had seen what no one else bothered to see. Of course, he always did. Detroit should've trusted his judgment. Wyld was hyperactive and forgot his clothes a lot, but damn. He doted on Micah—like seriously worshipped the ground Micah walked on. Detroit couldn't begin to fathom what that must feel like. Not only had he never had that, he never would.

Detroit rushed through his shower, trying not to dwell on that thought. Those musings always led back to one place. Payne. Detroit shook off the name as it floated through his mind. As he dressed, he did his best to keep his mind blank. There was this seed of hatred that was slowly growing inside Detroit. It had started out as hurt before turning to resentment, and then, one day he'd wondered if he didn't hate Payne a little. Everyone chose someone else over him. The worst part was, they always chose someone that left Detroit as the bad guy if he balked. His parents had chosen Jesus. Payne had chosen his son. Detroit was left with all this unrequited love and bitterness. He didn't know where to go with it. The emotions boiled in his gut, making him hurt and angry all the goddamn time. Detroit stared at the wall, getting lost in his downhill spiral and going to the place that almost killed him last time. He couldn't stop.

"Are you okay?" The quietly spoken words cut through Detroit's bleak thoughts.

"What?" he asked as he turned toward the door. Micah stood in the doorway, looking unsure of his welcome.

"Cortland said he was supposed to take you to your car, so you can go out, but he's been waiting almost two hours."

Detroit blinked. That wasn't possible. His gaze swung to the clock. It was nine fifteen. "Um." He didn't understand how that happened. "I guess I lost track of time. Fuck. I feel like shit for making him wait that long."

Micah's smile was everything light and sweet.

"It's okay. I sent him on and told him I'd take you if you still wanted to go."

Detroit shook his head. "I think I'll stay in." He blinked, still trying to come to terms with losing two hours. "I'm not sure what happened."

Wyld burst into the room, looking ready to take on the world. "Did I hear you say you're staying in again? I can't have that. Put your shirt on. We're going to my club."

"You own a club?" Even Detroit heard the disbelief in his voice.

"I own everything," Wyld said, sounding as if it should've been understood. And, really, it should have been. The real estate tycoon owned more property than anyone Detroit had ever met.

Micah's excitement pulled Detroit back on topic. He looked ready to bounce in place. "Yes, Detroit. You have to come with us."

"I'm not sure I'm ready to drink again," Detroit admitted.

With a shrug, Micah picked up Detroit's shirt from the bed and pulled it over his head, dressing him like a child. "I don't drink, and I still have a blast. You're coming and that's final." His smile grew. "We'll have so much fun, dancing all night. We haven't done that in forever."

"So, now I have to dance sober. That sucks."

"It won't. I promise," Micah said, looking too hopeful for Detroit to say no.

He sighed. "Fine. Let's go."

Micah clapped, looking like a little kid. "Yay! I promise you'll have fun."

Detroit had his doubts, but there was nothing he wouldn't do to keep Micah smiling, even if it meant making an ass of himself on the dance floor. Three hours later, Detroit's lungs burned, his legs ached, and his smile wouldn't abate. Wyld was a complete goofball who obviously couldn't care less what anyone thought, and it was catching. Detroit had danced every single dance with the pair without slowing. Wyld was bare from the waist up and covered in sweat. It amazed Detroit how Wyld had paid equal amounts of attention to Micah and him, yet anyone who looked could see his heart belonged to Micah. Detroit wanted to be jealous of their love, but he couldn't.

The music slowed. Pain immediately sliced through his chest. Detroit glanced around. The exclusive members' only club was huge and packed, but the floor cleared as the first love song floated through the air. The only people left on the dance floor were the couples. Detroit turned away, ready to leave Micah and Wyld alone. Wyld and Micah reached for him simultaneously. They towed him closer. He found himself pressed between them. They held on as they swayed to the music. The hint of sadness that sneaked in with the love song disappeared in their hold. For the first time in months, he felt stronger—like he might survive. Detroit knew exactly what he needed to do. It was time to start moving forward.

FOUR

THE PEOPLE WHO KNEW WHAT PAYNE DID FOR A living thought he had sex all day. That was a joke. He provided a service. His club ran—for the most part—without his interference while he sat here, balancing the books and ensuring people paid their membership fees. It was boring work, but it was his.

Something stirred in the air—like a minuscule zap of electricity. Payne lifted his chin. Detroit stood in the doorway, leaning against the frame. His hands were in the pockets of low-slung jeans. They looked worn and cupped the man's every asset. His maroon shirt looked thin and faded in spots, but the material stretched across the sexiest cut muscles. Payne's mind blanked. An unsure looking smile touched Detroit's amazing lips before falling away again. Payne had nothing. No words came.

"My membership card still works," Detroit said, explaining his presence as if he expected he'd be thrown out.

Payne forced his tongue to work. "I never suspended your account." He couldn't. That would mean they were over. They'd never be over.

Detroit's blue gaze never wavered from Payne. Payne wondered if his chest would explode. "Is it okay if I come in?"

Payne nodded toward the chair across from him. "Please."

Detroit sat. He wiped his palms on his thighs, showing his nervousness. "I'm headed back to Vegas today." The announcement was like a sledgehammer to the throat. Detroit didn't stop. "Even though I know..." Detroit stopped. His gaze skirted away. Something sad passed over his features. "I wanted to say goodbye."

Payne stood and moved to Detroit's side of the desk. After sitting on the edge, he pulled Detroit to his feet. "Come here," he said, gently tugging Detroit into his embrace. His heart squeezed so hard he thought he'd die when Detroit hugged him back. His familiar scent filled Payne's nose. Before he could stop himself, Payne's lips brushed Detroit's shoulder. "Stay." The whispered plea was out there before Payne could stop it.

Detroit quickly backed out of his hold. A deep line appeared between Detroit's eyebrows like he choked on unhappiness. "I can't do this."

Payne held up his hands. "You're not doing anything."

Detroit's mouth lifted in one corner in a sardonic smile before quickly falling away. "Yes, I am. I could've left without seeing you, but I chose to torture myself instead."

Payne tried staying calm. Detroit didn't need his judgement. "Seeing me is torture?"

Detroit still wouldn't look at him. He gave a jerky nod. "See, I know exactly where I went wrong. I fell in love with you." Detroit's gaze finally met his as he added, "Hard. I loved you too soon. Too much. At all. You didn't deserve it because you felt nothing for me. But the worst part of it all is, I loved you more than I loved me, which doesn't take much. Not really, but I let it destroy me." Detroit kept talking as if his every word wasn't choking the life from Payne. "I let it eat at my brain, until loving you picked apart everything good." Detroit looked away and blinked rapidly, as if fighting back tears. He cleared his throat. "I guess I thought if I said a proper goodbye this time..." He shrugged.

He'd known. It had been there in the back of Payne's mind. Detroit's suicide attempt had been his fault. The man had almost died because Payne's love was poison. Always had been. He twisted people until they no longer knew themselves. Payne straightened away from the desk. He took a deep breath.

"Kiss me then, and make this a proper goodbye."

Detroit's gaze locked on his. He didn't appear to as much as breathe.

Payne took a step, slowly closing the distance between them. "This way, you can look back on me fondly before you pack me away and move on. In fact, let's do this." Payne closed his office door and urged Detroit's back against it. "We can redo our last goodbye." Payne wanted to stop. Detroit looked ready to break—like the least little thing would shatter him. Because he was toxic, Payne kept going, pushing Detroit to the edge. He brushed his knuckles down Detroit's jaw. "I'll miss you, but I know being sponsored by Zander Kapra is every fighter's dream. You'll be great." Payne's gaze moved over Detroit's face, memorizing every detail. "You've always been amazing and way too good for an old man like me. It's good you've decided not to let me hold you back any longer."

"What are you doing?" Detroit asked, sounding strained.

Payne swallowed past the choking sensation of his heart breaking. "I'm giving you the goodbye you deserved the first time. Now, tell me you'll miss me and think of me occasionally, but you've outgrown me."

The muscle in Detroit's jaw jumped. His gaze shone bright with unshed tears and barely suppressed rage. "Please stop."

"I'll think of you too," Payne said, incapable of giving in. "When you're super famous and everyone knows your name, I'll tell everyone I once loved you and no one will believe."

"I said stop," Detroit yelled, shoving him away.

All the pain, anger, and helplessness he'd felt since losing Detroit and Detroit almost dying, exploded from Payne. He reclaimed the space between them, going chest to chest with Detroit. "You can leave, but I won't be forgotten," Payne promised as he captured Detroit's lips.

Detroit kissed him back every bit as fiercely. Their tongues stroked as if they were meant to touch.

Hunger slammed into Payne. Detroit shoved him away.

"I intend to do just that," Detroit said hotly as he ripped open the door and walked away. He was gone before the words sank in. Detroit planned to never think of Payne again. It was what he deserved. That didn't mean Payne intended to let Detroit go that easily. Detroit could walk away, but he couldn't leave Payne behind. Payne wasn't having it.

DETROIT FUMED. He shouldn't have gone to see Payne. Before driving in that direction, he'd known it was a mistake. But there was this stupid part of his heart that refused to be denied. It wouldn't accept they were over. While sitting in his car and staring at nothing, Detroit questioned his every life decision. If only he'd never touched Payne that first time. Maybe if he'd accepted Wyld's offer for a sponsorship over a year ago things would've been different. The biggest what if of all barged in and refused to budge. If only he'd died the way he'd wanted. Detroit wouldn't try harming himself again. He realized he was lucky to have survived and he couldn't hurt Micah like that. At the time, he hadn't considered anyone else's feelings. In truth, he'd fully believed they'd all be better off without him. Now, Detroit didn't know anything anymore. His phone buzzed, putting the brakes on his black thoughts.

Micah: *I love you, sweetie. It's selfish, I know, but I already miss you and wish you'd stay here.*

A smile tugged at the corners of Detroit's mouth. Micah was always like the sunshine, charging in and brightening everything with no say so from anyone. Detroit chewed his bottom lip. He was tempted. Going to Vegas meant returning to his solitude. That wasn't good for his mental health, but he couldn't rely on Micah forever. Micah was married to Wyld now, and he loved Micah. It wasn't fair for Detroit to keep hanging around, eating up Micah's free time.

Detroit: *I love you too. You're the most unselfish person I know. It's time for me to take my life back. Who knows? I might really be famous one day.*

Micah: *You've got this. Don't forget me.*

Detroit: *Not possible.*

The passenger side door opened as Detroit hit send. His head whipped up. Payne climbed inside. His jaw was set in a hard line, fascinating Detroit against his will. He didn't stop moving until his mouth covered Detroit's. Detroit sat, holding his phone between his hands, and accepting Payne's kiss. In his head, he recognized he should shove Payne away again. His heart paralyzed him. Payne's kiss was the most amazing experience in the world. It was the perfect combination of biting, searching, and sucking. He kissed like a man who could and would fulfill every fantasy. From the first time Payne kissed him, Detroit had been completely addicted. The man's kiss wove a spell, hypnotizing Detroit. Payne could ask for anything. Detroit was his.

Payne brushed another light kiss across Detroit's lips before settling down in the passenger's seat. He buckled his seat belt.

"Drive."

Detroit shifted the car into drive. "Where to?"

"My house."

Detroit pointed the vehicle in that direction and drove. He carefully kept his mind blank. Thoughts were his enemy. Tomorrow, he'd be back in Vegas. He could think all the thoughts then. Right now, Payne's kiss still lingered on his lips, making them tingle and all his worries disappear.

At Payne's house, he parked in his usual spot outside the first garage bay. He locked the truck and followed Payne to the back door. Even as Payne led him inside, Detroit refused to acknowledge the reason they were there. Tomorrow was soon enough. What did one more memory matter?

Payne locked the door behind them and toed off his shoes. Detroit followed his lead, kicking out of his as well. Payne took his hand and headed down the hall. The silence between them was so thick, it weighed heavy on Detroit's eardrums. Even as Payne's large bed came in to view, Detroit still shielded his mind from considering where this would go.

The moment they cleared the bedroom door, Payne turned. Detroit tilted his chin up and held Payne's stare. Payne cupped his face. His thumbs stroked Detroit's jawline. A singular thought sneaked its way through Detroit's mind. Payne was his everything.

Detroit didn't realize he'd reached for Payne until his hands slid across the man's hips. By then, it was too late to change his mind. He urged Payne closer. Payne dipped his chin. Detroit met him halfway. Their lips touched. They shared each other's air as Payne eased Detroit's shirt up. He leaned away, giving Payne permission to steal the material even as he tugged at Payne's shirt too. The instant they were both nude from the waist up, their lips met again. This time, so did their bare chests.

Detroit sucked in a gasp at the contact. Every inch of him felt overly sensitive. Payne's fingertips slowly traveled down Detroit's back as he stroked Detroit's tongue with his. Goosebumps rose on his skin. Payne followed Detroit's waistband around until his hands met at the button. Detroit's jeans loosened. The sound of his zipper sliding down seemed unnaturally loud. Payne undressed him. Slowly. Methodically. Not once did Detroit consider telling him no. It felt like it took forever before Payne's nude body covered his in bed, yet their time together flew. Detroit recognized their timer was ticking down. Soon, there would be hundreds of miles between them. They'd still be over, but this time without the hate-filled goodbye.

Detroit couldn't remember a single time Payne had made love to him. They'd always come together in a heated rage of passion. This was different. He was only vaguely aware of Payne suiting up and coating him with lube. It was like Payne's kisses were rendering him incompetent. Even though Detroit's cock leaked and begged for attention, his body's needs took a backseat to his emotions. His broken heart soaked up the attention, feeding off Payne's every touch. Payne's mouth moved from Detroit's lips to his neck as he pushed his way inside. Detroit fought for air. He held tight to Payne as Payne slowly pumped inside him. He kept such a tight hold on Detroit that each thrust rocked his entire body. It went on and on until Detroit forgot where Payne ended, and he began. Not a word was spoken. Even as the building pressure became an explosion of body quivering ecstasy, Detroit didn't make a sound.

Instead, he stole every kiss and touch he could fit into one afternoon. He stared at Payne in silence as Payne's orgasm hit. Detroit memorized every muscle twitch and facial expression. He took note of the exact color of Payne's flushed cheeks, and the way it brightened his eyes. The way his lips looked while swollen from Detroit's kisses. It was the first time in his life he'd known it would be the last. His eyes burned from the effort it took to hold back his tears. The swelling in his throat made speaking impossible. For the first time, Detroit understood everything. Payne loved him but would never publicly claim him. He would never hear the words fall from Payne's sexy full lips. Payne would never hold his hand in public. They were a bright explosion of emotion with no place in the world. This was the last memory they'd ever make together, and Detroit had to find a way to let him go.

FIVE

THE BAR INSIDE THE HOTEL WAS DEAD. THERE
were a few people scattered throughout, but the
lights were low, and no one spoke. Detroit stared at
his shot glass filled with whiskey. He didn't want it.
Not really. Detroit was simply following his usual
destructive pattern. There was no one here to stop
him. Still, he couldn't bring himself to drink.

"Let me guess. You're thinking of throwing away
your sobriety."

Detroit glanced over as the man claimed the bar
stool beside him. His long dark blond hair was a
mess, and he wore sunglasses even though the place
was barely lit.

"No," Detroit said, going back to staring at
his drink.

A low chuckle floated through the air and caressed Detroit's ears. It was a sexy sound. "You can't leave me guessing. I've been watching you stare at that drink for twenty minutes. Since I'm a storyteller at heart, I've come up with a dozen scenarios in my head. Now, I must know."

The man's deep Cajun accent had Detroit focusing on the guy once more. The moment the man had Detroit's attention, he plucked off his sunglasses and dropped them on the bar. Detroit barely stopped himself from looking away. The dude's eyes were beautiful. They were such a light green color, Detroit couldn't think of a way to describe them. Detroit smiled, fighting the urge to become the fake person he always was. "The last time I drank, I did something really stupid. I'm not sure I trust myself to drink again."

A bright smile lit the man's face. "Every time I drink, I do stupid shit." Before Detroit could guess at his intentions, the guy snatched up the shot and tossed it back. "There," he said, obviously speaking around the burn. "Temptation neutralized. I'm Omen," he said, holding out a hand for Detroit.

Detroit accepted. "Detroit. Can I buy you another drink?"

Omen tossed him a wink. "Nah, I swore off liquor years ago."

Detroit nodded toward the empty shot glass. "That says otherwise."

"That was nothing," Omen said, waving off Detroit's claim. "A rescue mission at best."

Detroit's smile was out of his control. It was nice to not be alone. "So, what's your story Omen? Why are you watching other people drink, or not drink?"

Omen looked around. "I like hotel bars. They're the perfect place to work," he said, tapping a leather-bound notebook Detroit hadn't noticed earlier. "Lots of interesting people frequent bars, especially during the day. It never fails to get my creative juices flowing."

"You're a writer?"

Omen shrugged. "A songwriter, among other things. You really don't know who I am, do you?"

Detroit eyed him. He did look somewhat familiar, but Detroit couldn't place him. "There's something familiar about you, but no, sorry."

The smile Omen wore grew. "Shit, man. Don't apologize. It's nice to have someone want to talk to me without even knowing me. Would you like to move to a table?"

"I would," Detroit said, meaning it. It was nice having someone to talk to, period.

Omen popped his sunglasses on the top of his head and picked up his notebook. "Cool."

Detroit watched the man as he headed for the nearest table. He was tall. At five-nine, a lot of men were taller than Detroit, but Omen was at least six-three. He was also skinny—like he never ate or stopped moving. The man had a rockstar vibe. It hit him. "Holy shit," he said, incapable of stopping himself as he claimed a chair at the table. "It's Omen Birch, right?"

The happiness in Omen's smile dimmed a hair. "Guilty."

Detroit immediately wished he'd pretended not to recognize him. "Sorry. That wasn't a holy shit can I have your autograph. It was more of a holy shit I'm stupid for not recognizing you sooner."

The sexy laugh was back. "It's okay. You still agreed to sit with me before you realized who I am. I'm taking it as a win."

Detroit imagined Omen didn't go anywhere he wasn't recognized. In fact, he was surprised the guy wasn't getting mobbed right now. As the lead singer of a famous metal band, Slight Bastards, Detroit expected to be assaulted by a mob of screaming fans at any moment. He had to know. "How are you getting away with sitting in peace at a bar?"

Omen shrugged. "It's Vegas. Everyone is a star. Plus, not a lot of people hang out in hotel bars in the daytime. They're all at the casino. What do you do, Mr. Detroit?"

A smile pulled at Detroit's lips at Omen's conversational tone. "I'm a fighter. MMA bet fights," he added for clarification. "The owner of this hotel is sponsoring me. That's the biggest reason I'm hanging out at the bar in the middle of the day. I pretty much eat, sleep, and work under this one roof."

Omen set his elbow on top of his notebook and propped up his chin, giving Detroit his full attention. "I've never met a fighter before, but I see it now. You have the physique and the scars."

Detroit moved his arms from the table to his lap. He didn't want Omen to know that side of him. For once, someone knew nothing about him and it was nice.

Omen wasn't having it. "Tell me all about yourself, Detroit. Are you from Detroit?"

An unexpected chuckle escaped him at Omen's playful tone. The man had a light behind his eyes. It was intelligence mixed with something Detroit couldn't quite place. Whatever it was, Detroit was like a moth, incapable of not moving closer to the flame. "No. I'm from Southern California. My parents met in Detroit. They both went to law school there. What about you? Is Omen your real name?"

"Yes, oddly enough. My parents are hippies."

Detroit couldn't hold back another laugh. He felt lighter than he had in... he didn't even know. Years, maybe. "Are you in town for a concert?"

"Yes, but not for two weeks. The guys and I decided we needed a little down time. We've been traveling a lot, and Vegas is always a fun town." He turned serious. His gaze moved over Detroit's face. "I have to say, I'm doubly glad we chose to stay here."

Detroit bit his bottom lip and fought a blush. It was a strange reaction that surprised even him. Detroit was accustomed to getting hit on. This was different. He couldn't explain it, but he didn't want to leave his spot next to Omen. "Would you like for me to pretend I've never heard of you and let you enjoy a nice vacation from being you?"

Omen hummed and tilted his chin at an angle as if thinking things over. "I'm not sure. On one hand, it's kind of nice to have someone choose to spend time with me just because. On the other hand, how will I ever tempt you to keep spending time with me if I'm no one? This is a quandary."

Despite Omen's joking tone, he got the feeling the man was serious. He didn't think Detroit would spend time with him if he wasn't famous. "Okay, complete stranger to me, would you like to have dinner with me?"

"I would like that," Omen said sounding serious. "But I hope that doesn't mean you're rushing off."

Detroit shook his head. "I'm not going anywhere. That was just me staking my claim for the rest of the day."

"If we'll be spending the next two weeks together, you should tell me why you're afraid to drink."

"Two weeks?" Detroit asked with a laugh. "Wow. That's a lot of assumption." His smile fell. "You're not the only one who likes the thought of hanging out with someone who doesn't know them."

Omen shrugged. "That only works when you don't want to know someone. I would, in fact, like to know you."

Fuck it. Maybe it was best Omen ran now before Detroit got attached. "The last time I had a drink, I tried to kill myself."

Omen didn't budge from his chin in hand and leaning toward Detroit stance. "Best you learn now that I'm a nosy fucker who must know every detail.

Why would someone as young and sexy as you are want to die?"

When Detroit had chosen to move to Vegas, part of his reasoning was that no one knew his name here. In Santa Clara, his name had once been all over the news. Everyone knew his story and knew he was a mess, but they didn't know, not really. Now, as he looked at Omen, he gave no fucks. It was almost a game to see if he could scare him away. "Are you sure you really want to hear this?"

Omen's smile was everything. It even lit his eyes. "I told you I'm a storyteller at heart. If you don't tell me, I'll be forced to make up my own version of events. You don't want that. I'll make you a drug addict or some shit."

Detroit winced. "You're right. I can't have you thinking that. Drugs aren't my vice. Hmmm, where to start," Detroit said, staring into space. He could say anything. Be anyone. Tell any lie. But the truth was so much easier to keep up with. Still, he couldn't look at Omen as he made his confessions. "When I was thirteen, I got busted by the police in the backseat with my homeroom teacher. Allison was twenty-four, and—now that I'm grown—I imagine quite fucked up. It was all over the news in my hometown. Coming from a heavily Christian home, my parents were mortified and blamed me, because —of course—they'd taught me better. I thought they were right to punish me because I thought I was grown and had made my choices. Now, of course, I realize I was a kid being manipulated by an adult."

"Agreed," Omen said, interrupting him. "Any adult should've realized a twenty-four-year-old woman wouldn't want a thirteen-year-old boy unless she was screwed in the head."

Detroit nodded. It felt good to have someone get that. No one had said that when he should've heard it years ago. "Anyhow, they brought down the hammer. I wasn't allowed to have friends. Go out. Do anything besides playing sports at school until I met Micah."

Omen held up his hand, halting Detroit. "Hold that thought." He stood and moved to the bar, ordering them waters before rejoining Detroit. He set one glass in front of Detroit. "Okay. Please continue. Who is Micah?"

Just the sound of Micah's name made Detroit smile. "He's my best friend. Micah is probably one of the most beautiful men in the world, but he gives off an angelic vibe that can be felt for miles. He does volunteer work and helps the homeless. My parents were overjoyed to meet him. So, they loosened the reins. As long as I was with Micah, I could do whatever I wanted. It helped that Micah lived with a single father. You know, no more older women for me to seduce." Detroit brought the glass to his lips. He needed something to wash down his bitterness. "For a few years, everything looked a little brighter. But I still had that pallor hanging over me. It was like everyone's eyes were always on me, judging me. Micah was the only bright spot."

"So, you fell in love with the angel."

A snort escaped Detroit. He couldn't help it. Micah would die if he'd heard that. "No. I mean, I do love Micah, but not like that. It's hard to explain. For years, I'd been punished for thinking I was in love with an adult. Then, I spent every waking moment with this perfect guy my age, and I didn't want him. I mean, Micah didn't want me either, but that never factored in my mind."

A part of Detroit wanted to bite off his tongue to stop himself from talking. Omen was a stranger, and Detroit was telling the man his every secret. He couldn't stop. Omen looked truly interested, and Detroit needed the words out of his head.

"I found myself with another taboo fixation, and I realized my parents were right to blame me. It is me. But I didn't want to mess up my life or hurt my parents again, so I became this huge flirt. I tried very hard not to want who I wanted. To find *anyone* else. The harder I fought myself, trying not to be this gigantic disappointment, the more I failed myself."

"You said your parents are extremely religious, so I'm assuming it didn't help matters that who you wanted is a man," Omen said, interrupting again.

Detroit smiled. There was no happiness or humor in the gesture. It was all bitterness. Years and years of bitterness. "It didn't help matters that who I wanted was Micah's father."

Omen's eyebrows rose. He sat back. "Whoa."

There it was. The building distaste. The sudden realization that Detroit was a bad person. Despite the fact he'd been digging for that reaction and knew it would come, Detroit's throat still swelled. There was something wrong with him. Everyone saw it. He craved things he shouldn't. There was something broken inside him.

To Detroit's surprise, Omen shook off whatever he was thinking and went back to leaning on the table with his chin cupped in his hand. "So, this suicide attempt, was it because you won him, or because you didn't?"

Detroit swallowed past the pain. "It was because I lost him, and Micah, and me. My cup is empty and shattered. I keep searching for something to fill me up. Take away the emptiness, but a broken glass won't hold water. It's exhausting."

A sweet smile touched Omen's lips. "I'm glad we met, Detroit."

The comment surprised a laugh from Detroit. "I can't imagine why."

"Are you serious?" Omen asked, sounding scandalized. "I've gotten to spend my afternoon talking with a sexy younger man with a poetic soul who likes older men. This is like hitting the jackpot. I can't wait to spend the next two weeks getting to know everything about you."

The air lightened. Detroit let the pressure suffocating him melt away. Maybe Omen was crazy for sticking around after Detroit dumped his baggage on him. If so, he was the kind of crazy that Detroit needed more of in his life. The next two weeks looked brighter already.

WITH HIS FEET crossed at the ankle and resting on his desk, Payne stared at nothing. Twice, people had knocked on his office door. Payne hadn't bothered answering. Nothing mattered anymore.

Each day, he got up, dressed, and came to work. He went through the motions, barely eating. Just surviving. The only thought in his head was the last time he saw Detroit.

He'd hoped if he made slow love to Detroit, then he'd survive the fall when Detroit left. But the memory of kissing Detroit and owning his body wasn't what lingered, choking the life from Payne. It was the vision of Detroit dressing to leave him. Detroit hadn't once looked Payne's way. Payne hadn't said a word. Inside his head, he'd been screaming for Detroit to look at him. To see he was drowning without him. To fucking stay. Instead, he'd lain there in impotent silence, because he couldn't escape the truth. Detroit was better off without Payne. Payne knew Detroit would've stayed if he'd asked, but that wasn't fair. Detroit was young and had the brightest future ahead of him. Payne was old enough to be his father and was twisted all the way to his soul. The kindest thing he'd ever done was let Detroit leave. But, fuck if it wasn't killing Payne. Every day, a little more of Payne faded away.

Another knock landed on his closed office door. Payne rubbed the center of his chest, trying to scrub away the ache where Detroit had been ripped from

Payne's soul. He wondered if he'd ever care about anything again.

"Dad, please open the door."

Payne's head snapped toward the door so fast he almost gave himself whiplash. He shot to his feet. No goddamn way Micah was inside his club. Whoever let that happen would die. Payne ate up the floor between his desk and the door. He ripped it open. Sure enough, his son's sweet smile and angelic face blinked up at him with his large doe eyes. Payne wanted to roar his rage. Micah always took the wind from his sails.

"Baby, what are you doing here? You know I don't want you inside this place."

Micah's gaze never wavered from his. His shoulders lifted. "You haven't answered any of my calls and texts. I was worried."

Payne waved Micah inside his office and closed the door before he caught sight of anything he shouldn't. It didn't matter that Payne knew Micah was grown. He would always be Payne's innocent baby. "I forgot my phone at home."

As Micah claimed a seat at his desk, Payne automatically scanned the room, looking for anything he didn't want Micah to see. He'd always tried to keep his life separated into two parts—a normal home life for Micah and this place. Nothing jumped out at him.

Rather than reclaiming the chair behind his desk, Payne grabbed a folded chair that leaned against the wall and set it close to Micah. "Is everything okay?" Payne asked the second he was settled.

Micah nodded, but he worried at his bottom lip, belying his answer. "It's just that Detroit has been back in Vegas three days now and I haven't heard from him. I get that he doesn't feel close to me anymore and that he's fallen out of the habit of checking in, but still. Then, I started calling and texting you and you didn't answer either. My nerves are on edge." Micah deflated as he made the confession.

Payne nodded along. His chest tightened with each word. When Detroit had left town, Payne had known he'd never hear from the man again. As much as he wanted to make peace with that, hearing Micah's panic made it impossible. "I'd try calling him, but he's twice as unlikely to answer me."

Somehow, Micah's shoulders managed to droop an inch lower. "Wyld is the best husband on the planet, but he won't understand if I run after Detroit after only three days, or possibly at all. I don't know."

Yeah, Payne would imagine no husband would

understand that. "Tell me how to fix it. I don't want you stressing over this."

Micah went back to chewing his bottom lip. His gaze moved over Payne's face, as if searching for something only he could see. Micah's chest expanded on a deep breath. "Can I ask you a question?"

Payne didn't hesitate. "Of course."

"Do you love him?"

The question shut down Payne's brain. "I'm sorry. What?"

"Detroit," Micah said, as if Payne didn't understand. "I mean, when I first realized there was something between you two, I thought it was physical. Because, well, you're you and Detroit..." Micah looked slightly guilty. He cleared his throat, and the guilt disappeared from his expression. "Anyhow, after Vegas, I think maybe it's more, but I need to hear it."

The thing was, if it had been anyone else, Payne would've shut this shit down quick. No one discussed his personal life. It was Micah. Not only was Micah Payne's whole reason for existing, Micah was also Detroit's best friend. For those reasons—the same rationale that had torn Payne and Detroit apart —Payne had to be honest now.

74

Payne cleared his throat. Saying yes didn't seem enough, but neither did he know where to start. "On Detroit's twenty-second birthday, you two had dinner and then you set him free to go party because you were too young to drink." Plus, Micah wasn't a bar hopper, thank god. Payne cleared his throat again, wishing he didn't feel so damn guilty for falling for someone way younger than him who also happens to be his son's best friend. "Instead, he met me at a hotel." Only the fact that Micah didn't even flinch kept Payne talking. "By that time, we'd already been seeing each other close to a year. I asked Detroit what he wanted for his birthday, giving him pretty much carte blanche to demand anything from me. He didn't answer right away. While I waited, this traitorous voice sounded in the back of my mind. As I stared at him, I realized I was hoping against hope that he would put his foot down and demand that I stop keeping him a secret." A sad smile tugged at Payne's lips as he recalled that moment. "I knew he'd never ask for that, because he loves you too much to hurt you. But I realized I wanted him to love me too much to hide."

"What did he ask for?"

Micah's question caught him off guard. Payne turned his face away as a lump formed in his throat.

"Detroit wouldn't want you to know. I guess, what I'm getting at is—yes. I love him, but sometimes that's not enough to cover the costs."

To his surprise, Micah took his hand, forcing his gaze back Micah's way. "Love doesn't care about anyone's feelings. It doesn't care that I'm your son or Detroit is my friend. Yes, I was upset when I noticed how you look at each other. But, honestly, my reasons have nothing to do with you. Many times, I've felt very alone and like Detroit was the only person who understood me. It was like all that was going away. I'm glad you love Detroit. He needs something I can't give him. I get the feeling you can though." Micah squared his shoulders. "So, if I paid for you to go after him, would you?"

A snort escaped Payne before he could call it back. "First off, I don't need you to pay for anything. Secondly, it doesn't matter how I feel. Detroit is finished with me. Third, loving someone isn't enough. It won't make me twenty-four years younger or matters less complicated. Love definitely won't undo the horrible way things ended or the fact that my career makes me impossible to love. There are so many things standing between us."

Micah shrugged, blowing off Payne's excuses. "So? Most of that is either in your mind or unimportant. I didn't think anyone would ever love me, and I was wrong. You are too." Micah made a sweeping gesture with his arm. "This place, well, it's places like this and the way times are in general that make me less appealing in everyone's eyes, but Detroit isn't like me. I'm willing to bet he never once fought with you over owning this place."

That was true. Detroit was more likely to play with him here than complain. Still. "I'm not sure Detroit wants me to chase him. In fact, I'm pretty certain the move to Vegas was all about leaving me behind."

Micah snorted. "Detroit isn't known for making the best decisions." Micah's expression turned serious. "He needs you. I'm sorry I didn't say as much sooner."

Payne didn't know what to say. He wanted to go after Detroit, but he wasn't sure that Detroit wanted him any longer.

Micah didn't let up. "If you get there and things don't work out, I promise I'll never bring it up again. But if you don't go because you think you know Detroit's mind better than he does, I'll never forgive you."

Payne's eyebrows hit his hairline. "Whoa, you're bringing out the big guns here."

Micah's smile was unrepentant. "It seems someone has to."

"Okay." Payne cut off Micah's triumph before it grew too big. "However, if I get there and see he's better off without me, I'm not forcing my way into his life."

"Fair enough," Micah said, trying for serene and failing miserably. He obviously gave up and a huge grin appeared. "I love you."

Fuck. Micah made it impossible to be irritated with him. "I love you too, goddam it," he grumbled. He only had one son. Despite being grown, Payne swore the boy would be the death of him.

SIX

A LOUD KNOCK SOUNDED ON DETROIT'S HOTEL room door. Detroit spent a second staring at it. He wasn't expecting anyone. In fact, he was down to his workout shorts and ready for bed. He still got tired faster than he liked since his hospital stay. When the knock landed again, he moved to answer. It didn't seem whoever it was planned to leave him in peace.

Omen wore a smile and held a bottle of vodka on the other side. He didn't wait for Detroit to greet him. "So, I was thinking about your fear of drinking and came up with a plan."

Detroit bit back a grin. "Is that so?"

"It is. You need a trusted friend to keep your spirits up while you get plastered. That way, it's like mood control."

After taking a step back, Detroit waved him inside. "I'm not sure that's such a great idea, but you're welcome to come inside and hang out." Detroit closed the door and moved to sit on the bed.

Omen claimed the chair at the desk. He eyed Detroit a moment longer than necessary. "Goddamn. I know you said you're a fighter, but wow. I'm having some serious body envy and shit right now."

Heat climbed up Detroit's cheeks. Even he didn't know why. It wasn't like he didn't know how he looked. Detroit worked hard on his body. Still, something about Omen made him shy. It didn't help that—despite his flirtatious manner—Detroit was about eighty percent sure Omen was straight. When Omen gave compliments, they sounded like Detroit shouldn't take them to heart. "You shouldn't. Fighting is the only thing I'm good at. I don't really have a lot of talent or anything special, to be honest. You're a musical genius. That makes you way better than I'll ever be. Looks fade. What you have is forever."

Omen leaned back in his chair, looking like the sexy rock god he was, and smirked. "You have men and women tripping over themselves to be the one, don't you?"

A wave of sadness washed over Detroit. He

could lie and say it wasn't true, but he didn't want to. "They want the fake me. The me that I show to the world. The person I really am when I'm in a relationship, that version of me scares people, so I keep it hidden. So, no. I don't have anyone chasing after the real me."

Omen's smile fell. "Yeah, me too." He sounded serious and sad. Detroit wanted to hug him. Omen shook his head and his smile reappeared. His eyes brightened. "We should date and scare each other."

Since Omen cracked that door, Detroit decided to bust through like a cop on a raid. "Have you ever dated a man?"

Omen snatched up the vodka from where he'd left it on the desk. He cracked the seal and turned it up, not bothering with a glass. When he answered Detroit, he sounded like he was speaking through the burn. "Once."

"I never heard that rumor, and I thought you swore off alcohol."

"It was a secret," Omen said with a shrug. "And if we're going to talk about Keegan, I'm going to need a drink."

That was a sentiment Detroit understood too well. "Pass me that, and I'll tell you all about how

Payne owns a club called the Den of Payne. It's where we spent most of our time."

Omen passed the bottle Detroit's way as he moved to join Detroit on the bed. "This sounds interesting—like I'm about to find out why you're so terrifying to date."

Detroit turned up the bottle and drank down his fear. He'd never made this confession. Payne was the only one who knew. But Detroit was pretty sure, once Omen resumed his tour, Detroit would never see him again. That made it easier to spill his secrets. "The Den of Payne is exactly what it sounds like. Payne hurts people for money. For the right price, he'll make any fantasy come true, as long as no sex is involved. He's not a whore. He provides a service. Sex does take place there, but it has to be consensual and no money can change hands. It's like a members' only adult playroom."

"I've been to a similar establishment, so I get what you're saying."

Detroit nodded, thankful he didn't need to spell it out any further. "The minute I turned twenty-one and could join, I did. Not for the sex, but for Payne and what he provides."

Omen interrupted. "So, you like to hurt and that scares people."

"Yes," Detroit said, while doing his best to bite back his embarrassment. "But I chose Payne for more than that. I knew he wouldn't judge me when I asked him..." Detroit took another deep swig for fortification. "... to tell me all the things I wished my father would," Detroit finished without looking Omen's way. He'd never thought to confess that to anyone.

"I didn't ask Keegan to keep us a secret," Omen said fast, like ripping off a bandage, and saving Detroit's pride. "He asked me not to tell anyone we were together, because he didn't want his friends to think he was gay, and he damn sure didn't want them to know he was gay for a guy who likes to wear makeup and women's clothes."

At the confession, Detroit's shoulders relaxed. He passed the bottle Omen's way and settled back against the pillows. "That's a tough one." He eyed Omen's high cheekbones and full lips. "I bet you look damn sexy in makeup."

Omen shrugged. "I dress up and get dolled up for interviews and magazine spreads all the time. Since I've been doing so for years, I never thought it was that big of a deal. Then, I met Keegan, and it was such a big deal to him that it swallowed my life whole. Now, I don't know. It's like I'm nothing at all."

"What happened with Keegan?"

Omen turned up the bottle. "I realized he would never love me, so I bounced. He can find some other poor bastard to keep a secret, and he can keep telling himself he's not gay without me."

Detroit leaned closer to Omen, ensuring their shoulders touched. "I would be proud to be with you."

After shifting positions, Omen slung his arm across Detroit's shoulders and tucked him closer to his side. He took another drink before responding. "We'd make a beautiful couple. Everyone would be jealous."

Except, Omen felt like a friend, and Detroit needed one of those more than he needed another man. "Maybe one day, after I wrestle my heart away from Payne, I'll show you what it's like to be with someone who isn't ashamed of you."

Omen nodded. "Maybe someday Keegan won't be in my head, kicking the shit out of my heart any longer, and I'll take you up on that."

Maybe. Someday. Right now, all Detroit could do was drink and let Omen hold him, because every other second of the day, he belonged to Payne, and that shit hurt.

PAYNE TOOK A DEEP BREATH, hoping to calm his racing heart. As his knuckles landed on Detroit's door, he released the breath. He'd waited two days after Micah's request to make his way to Vegas. Payne couldn't walk away from his club without some planning. Now, here he was, completely ready to fuck up Detroit's life all over again. God help them both. Laughter and voices rumbled on the other side a half second before the door opened. Payne stared at a stranger. The man's long blond hair and light green eyes looked somewhat familiar. He was incredibly sexy. The guy was at least six-three. His flannel shirt hung open over a white t-shirt while his legs were encased in ripped jeans. Payne's gaze traveled down the man's length to the work boots he wore. Even though they looked worn, they were also designer brand. The dude had looks and money. There was something about him. It niggled at the back of Payne's mind, but Payne couldn't place him. He was too confused by his presence.

Payne glanced at the room number. "Sorry. I must have the wrong room."

"You're looking for Detroit, right?"

Payne nodded.

The guy opened the door wider, exposing Detroit deeper in the room. He was smiling. Payne's heart rate kicked up.

Detroit glanced his way, and his smile fell. "Payne?" he said, sounding confused, as he moved in Payne's direction. "Is everything okay?"

At the mention of his name, the guy between them perked up. He stared harder at Payne.

Payne ignored him and forced his lips into a smile. He hadn't expected Detroit to not be alone. "Yeah. I—"

"Micah sent you to check on me, didn't he?" Detroit asked, interrupting him.

"Actually, I came to take you to dinner."

That seemed to give Detroit pause. "You came all the way to Vegas to take me to dinner?"

The guy straightened away from the wall, looking amused. "That sounds like an amazing idea. Detroit, you should invite the man in, and I've got to be headed out. Big plans and lots of stuff to do... elsewhere. You know how it is."

Detroit looked panicked. "No. Omen, you don't have to go."

"It was nice to meet you, Omen," Payne said, taking control of the situation. "I'm sure you'll get everything you set out to do accomplished... elsewhere." Payne's voice hardened on the final word.

To his surprise, Omen's humor seemed to deepen. He stepped back and waved Payne into the room. Once Payne passed him, Omen didn't close the door. He focused on Detroit. "I'll check in later." His gaze slid Payne's way. "And you can tell me everything. Have a nice dinner, you two." Without waiting for a response, Omen left them alone, closing the door with a snap.

Payne eyed Detroit while Detroit stared at the closed door as if trying to decide what happened. Fuck. He was amazing. Beautiful. Payne didn't want to as much as blink. All he wanted to do was stare at him. Detroit was shirtless—like Payne had caught him in the middle of dressing to go out.

"You look gorgeous." The words were out before Payne gave himself permission to speak.

Detroit looked his way. "Why are you here?"

"I already told you why."

Detroit's expression gave nothing away beyond

his obvious confusion. "People don't go hundreds of miles for dinner."

Payne let the heat he felt at seeing Detroit seep into his stare. "I've found there's not much I wouldn't do for you."

Detroit turned away and pulled a shirt over his head. He turned back Payne's way as he dragged the material down his torso, stealing away the sight of his cut chest and sexy abs. His gaze stayed locked on his hands as he smoothed the material. "I don't want to go to dinner with you. If you didn't notice, I had company. I also had plans with Omen tonight."

Payne didn't back down. "If you didn't notice, Omen left. Now, you have plans with me."

"I'm not one of your clients," Detroit snapped, taking Payne by surprise. He held Payne's stare with defiance flashing in his eyes. "Not anymore. You don't get to push me away and then show up demanding your way as if nothing happened."

"Get your shoes on. I made reservations at one of the downstairs restaurants."

Detroit didn't budge. "I don't think you're hearing me."

Payne closed the distance between them, going flush against Detroit, cutting off his argument. The dresser stopped the man from getting away. "I don't think *you're* hearing *me*. Get your shoes on and go to dinner with me right now, or I can remove your clothes and you can get on your knees. Which will it be?"

Detroit's gaze never wavered from Payne's mouth. He licked his lips but made no move to touch Payne.

Detroit flattened his palm against Payne's chest. For a moment, Detroit stared at his hand. His fingers lightly caressed Payne. Then, he pushed, shoving Payne away from him. "I have other plans."

As Payne looked on, Detroit found a worn pair of work boots and shoved his feet inside. He headed for the door without bothering to tie them or looking Payne's way. Not a single word was spoken as he walked out, leaving Payne alone inside his room as if he didn't care if he stayed or went. A smile that felt evil even to Payne pulled at his lips. Detroit had played his first chess piece. The next move belonged to Payne.

THE MOMENT DETROIT was out the door, he pulled out his phone and sent Omen a text.

Detroit: *Where are we meeting?*

Omen: *You have a date.*

Detroit: *No. I made plans with you.*

Omen: *I won't turn you down if you prefer me. Third floor. Sudden Skies bar. Dancing is afoot.*

There was a quiver in Detroit's stomach that wouldn't abate. He tried calming himself during the elevator ride, but nothing changed. Payne was here. Left behind in Detroit's room. He couldn't take it. The knowledge was too much. The elevator door opened, setting him free on the third floor. The moment he cleared the club's door, he spotted Omen. Detroit kept his head held high as he headed for the dance floor. Even though he'd already had a little liquid fortification before joining the throng of gyrating bodies. Adrenaline was his true high tonight. His heart still raced from walking away from Payne. Detroit had never done that before. Payne was always the one to send him packing. Detroit felt stronger than ever before. He felt fucking invincible.

People surrounded Omen, fighting to be the one the man focused upon. The bodies seemed to part as Detroit hit the floor. Omen's light green gaze landed on Detroit and didn't budge. He smirked. A laugh rose in Detroit's throat and stuck. Omen opened his arms. Detroit slid his way in, matching Omen's rhythm. The music was too fast for slow dancing. Detroit still danced too close.

Omen's mouth touched the shell of his ear. "You look damn proud of yourself."

Detroit spoke loudly too, ensuring he was heard over the music. "I've never ditched Payne before."

Omen set his forearms on Detroit's shoulders and kept time with the music. "Doesn't look like you ditched him this time either."

Before Detroit could ask, Omen spun Detroit and molded against his back, gyrating against his ass. He kept one arm locked around Detroit's neck and his mouth pressed to Detroit's ear. To anyone watching, he was sure their dance looked intimate. In truth, Omen was keeping up their conversation and directing Detroit's gaze. "Third table to the left."

Detroit followed Omen's directions. Payne sat there, seemingly relaxed, drinking a beer and watching them.

Omen ran his hand down Detroit's chest and stomach, stopping at Detroit's waistband. "Should I make him jealous?"

"Careful," Detroit warned. "There'll be pictures of you dancing with me all over the tabloids tomorrow."

Omen somehow managed to shift even closer

and still keep time with the music. "Do you think I'm ashamed of being seen with you?"

Detroit wondered if Omen's tone would be different if Keegan caught wind of him with another man. He decided not to touch the question. Instead, he focused on Omen's earlier question. "Payne doesn't get jealous. He joins in instead."

"Damn," Omen said, sounding every bit as interested as any sane person would. "He is very sexual, isn't he? I can see him running a members' only playroom."

Detroit stared at Payne, seeing what everyone couldn't help but notice. There was something primal about Payne. It went beyond the wide shoulders, hard chest, tall frame, and exterior beauty. Sex dripped from Payne. Detroit couldn't explain it. He'd never met anyone else like him. With one glance Payne could make someone lose their clothes like—won't be needing these.

As he looked on, Payne came to his feet. Detroit couldn't tear his gaze away. He also couldn't stop moving to the music as if he danced only for Payne. The distance between them disappeared. Payne's body collided with his. He matched Detroit's pace. His mismatched gaze held Detroit's as his hands slipped beneath the hem of Detroit's shirt until he held Detroit's waist, skin on skin between his hands. Detroit had a hard time catching his breath. Both Payne and Omen were taller than him. He was sandwiched between them, giving him thoughts he didn't want.

For a moment, they simply moved to the music. Then, Payne snagged the back of Omen's neck and hauled him closer. He touched his lips to Omen's ear, keeping his words for only Omen. Detroit felt Omen go hard. He lost his breath at the sensation. There was no one Payne couldn't affect. Payne pulled away and focused on Detroit. He touched Detroit's jaw, keeping him from looking away. Payne dipped his head and captured Detroit's lips. It was a simple kiss. Payne sucked Detroit's bottom lip between his and then it was over.

"Later," he said barely loud enough for Detroit to hear, but he felt it all the way to his soul as Payne walked away. Detroit watched him go, fighting the urge to chase him even as he stared at Payne's sexy ass.

"Holy shit," Omen said, reminding him of his presence. "What just happened?"

"Told you he was a joiner," Detroit said, finding his words.

Omen wrapped his arms around Detroit's chest

and held on even as he kept dancing. "Not in this case," Omen said, surprising him. "He gave me a very detailed list of what the three of us could do together, and then he let me know in a very clear manner it would never happen, because you are his."

Omen's claim shocked Detroit enough that he turned in Omen's arms. "What?" Payne was never, ever possessive.

Omen nodded. "You're a lucky bastard. All that is yours alone. I'm thinking maybe you should chase after him."

Detroit shook his head. "I'm here with you."

An indulgent smile pulled at Omen's lips. "You're not, so be free. I'll still be around for another week. Go steal a night of happiness. Just because something might not be permanent doesn't mean it's not perfect or any less real."

Omen was right. He'd never looked back on Payne and thought it was all for the fun of it. Every second had been real, raw, and powerful, even as he'd known it wasn't meant to last. Why did tonight have to be any different?

Detroit went up onto his toes and kissed Omen's cheek. "Catch you later, babe."

Omen winked. "You know it." Omen turned away and chose another dance partner, freeing

Detroit. Detroit wasted no time heading for the door. Payne was here, and Detroit was his, even if it was only for one night.

PAYNE STARED at the closed elevator door, trying not to think. He had a room booked on the tenth floor for the next week. Seven days. That's how long Payne had to figure this out. Just over ten thousand minutes, give or take a few hundred, for Payne to make Detroit understand he loved him. Maybe he'd leave here empty handed, but at least he would know he tried. It was also possible Detroit was better off without him. Either way, Payne needed to know.

The elevator door opened. He stepped inside and turned to wait to be taken upstairs. Payne's breath caught. Detroit stepped inside as well. He held Payne's stare, not bothering to face the door as it closed behind him. Payne reached around him and hit the button to take him to the tenth floor. Detroit didn't budge, forcing Payne to invade his space to reach the buttons. Still, his gaze never wavered. Each breath came harder than the last as Payne took in Detroit's expression. Detroit had made up his mind. It was written on his face. The staring match continued until the door opened again.

"This is my floor."

Detroit dipped his chin, acknowledging Payne's words. "Lead the way."

With every step Payne took, he felt Detroit's presence at his back. When he reached his room, Detroit stood close enough that Payne could feel the heat radiating off his skin as he unlocked the door. One second, Payne felt the overwhelming peace of Detroit's presence, and then the door closed behind them. They were alone. Payne sprang. He tore at Detroit's shirt, peeling it from his skin. Their mouths clashed as they fought to be closer. Payne's body still burned from Detroit's teasing dance. Now, Detroit's touch added fuel to the flames. Payne bit into Detroit's skin, trailing bites down his neck and shoulder. They weren't light. He was dangerously close to tearing the skin. Detroit moaned like he was getting fucked.

"Goddamn, Payne. You'll make me come in my jeans if you keep that up."

"No," Payne growled, sounding inhuman even to his ears. "I want your cum in my mouth," he demanded as he dropped to his knees and tore at Detroit's jeans. He wasn't gentle as he set Detroit's erection free. Payne ensured his teeth scraped the man's cock as he swallowed him. Pre-cum hit his tongue. Detroit tugged at his hair, pulling him closer. Fucking his mouth. Payne treated him like a meal. He nipped as he sucked, intentionally hurting Detroit. Detroit cursed and writhed, unabashedly loving every second. There was no shame in their kinks when they were together. Each time he caused pain and Detroit moaned, Payne feared he'd be the one who blew in his jeans. He ripped open his zipper and palmed his cock, stroking as he sucked off Detroit.

Payne let Detroit slip almost from his mouth. He nipped at the man's sensitive crown before quickly taking him down his throat. A cry tore through the room. Hot cum filled Payne's mouth. He sucked and swallowed, taking his well-deserved treat. When he'd gotten every drop, he shot to his feet. He barely caught a glimpse of Detroit's dazed expression before he spun the man, slamming him face first against the hotel desk.

Payne slowed. His heart skipped a beat. He hadn't meant to be so rough. Without thought, he reversed course, pulling Detroit back to facing him. His panicked gaze swept Detroit's body, searching for damage.

"Oh my god. I'm so sorry. I got carried away."

Detroit shushed him. He cupped Payne's face, forcing him to hold his stare. "Stop, Payne. I'm fine. Look at me. I'm fine. Breathe." He took a deep breath, enticing Payne to follow his lead.

Payne did as told. He sucked in a deep breath.

"Good. Let it out."

Payne released his breath.

Detroit smiled. "There you go. Keep breathing. You would never hurt me for real. I know that. Even when you're in the zone, you've never caused me any harm. It's okay, baby. I'm okay."

Payne fell forward and wrapped Detroit in a tight embrace. His insides shook. He couldn't lose control. Detroit was too precious. "I'm sorry."

Detroit stroked his back. "My sweet baby. Please stop apologizing. You know I'm not helpless. I'd kick your ass if I ever thought you were out to harm me."

Detroit's claim surprised a chuckle from him. He knew Detroit could hold his own. The man got tossed around for a living. It was Payne. He needed the discipline. His sanity required he stay in control. He stroked Detroit, trying to make up for his earlier treatment. Their mouths sought each other like their minds were connected. That's who they were—two halves always seeking their stronger part.

PAYNE KISSED like the master he was. Detroit always lost himself when Payne's mouth was on his body. Detroit was weak when Payne wasn't around to keep him strong. Left to his devices, Detroit would always make bad decisions. Payne kept him on the right path, but Detroit knew Payne was scared as hell of himself. Without Detroit to reassure him, sometimes Payne was paralyzed by his intensity.

Detroit kept his kiss sweet and reassuring, enticing Payne away from the edge in his mind. Payne's kiss lightened even more.

"Let me try again," he begged against Detroit's lips. "I won't hurt you."

There was never a doubt. Detroit wasn't scared of Payne ever harming him physically. Emotionally was a different story. Payne held the strings of Detroit's heart together. With the smallest cut in the right place, Detroit would completely unravel.

"Tell me where you want me. I'm yours."

Payne stroked Detroit's shoulders and chest while eyeing his face, as if assuring himself Detroit was really okay. He gave Detroit a sharp nod. "I'll slow down."

Detroit bit back a smile. He didn't know how he

could be expected not to love Payne. It wasn't fair for anyone, even Payne, to think he could resist. Payne peeled off the remaining stitches of Detroit's clothing before stripping off his own. Detroit had more patience than usual due to Payne blowing his mind. Still, as Payne traced the line separating his abs, Detroit found it harder to breathe.

"I know I've told you hundreds of times, but you're so fucking beautiful. It never stops humbling me that you would want me."

He didn't understand why Payne always said such things. Payne was gorgeous. He was tall with wide shoulders—like a brick wall. Yet, he was still soft in a way Detroit couldn't explain. Maybe he only saw what he wanted.

Payne linked his fingers through Detroit's. He tugged him toward the bed. As Detroit looked on, Payne pulled down the covers. He sat down and towed Detroit forward, urging him to straddle Payne's hips. Detroit wrapped his arms around Payne's neck. He held the man's stare. As Payne's arms encircled him, some of the man's intensity returned. "I'm lonely without you."

Detroit's eyes stung. He'd ever expected such a confession from Payne.

Payne didn't stop. "Nothing is the same with you

gone. The only thing that saves my sanity is knowing you're alive somewhere in the world. Just the knowledge you exist, that's all I need. So, you can't stop, okay?"

It was the closest Payne would ever come to addressing his suicide attempt, Detroit knew. "I'm okay. I won't go anywhere."

Payne nodded. "There are condoms and lube in that bag behind you. I want you to get me ready to go, and then I want you back in this position."

Detroit climbed from Payne's lap to do as told. He found the items and returned to Payne's side. With more enthusiasm and touching than necessary, Detroit rolled a condom down Payne's sexy, thick cock. He concentrated on keeping his breathing steady as he coated the sheath with lube. It didn't help his lung function that Payne looked ready to explode. His lips were swollen, and his cheeks were flushed. Heat blasted from his gaze as he watched Detroit work. His stare made Detroit feel sexy and powerful. He made a show of climbing back into Payne's lap.

His fingers encircled Payne's cock. He positioned the man's erection and impaled himself. His breath left his lungs as Payne stretched him wide. He tried to hold still and adjust. A sound escaped Payne that was filled with such sexy longing that Detroit couldn't wait. He lifted and rode Payne's dick. Their locked gazes never wavered. That scary connection they had was in its full glory.

Payne's lips parted. His breaths quickened. Detroit couldn't look away. He pushed, shoving Payne onto his back. Payne moaned as Detroit held all the control, fucking Payne's hard dick the way he liked. He knew it was hard for Payne to let him be in charge, so Detroit ensured his man knew nothing but pleasure.

Detroit tilted his head back and sucked air. Payne felt amazing inside him. It seemed one cock should be the same as any other, but there was no one like Payne for Detroit. He was the perfect fit.

Payne touched him every place he could reach and stroked Detroit's erection. "You're always hard for me, no matter how many times I make you come. It messes with my head. You're like the most intense drug, keeping me higher than I've ever been. Fuck me, sexy. Make me fly."

Detroit couldn't concentrate on anything other than the tugging on his cock and the way Payne moved inside him. He was like a spring being wound tighter and tighter. Even breathing became secondary. His muscles tensed. He reached for the ecstasy Payne offered. Pleasure slammed into him. Jets of cum coated Payne's body beneath him. Payne shouted. His body shook. He collapsed in a heap into Payne's waiting arms. Payne rolled and tucked Detroit beneath him. His mouth covered Detroit's. These moments were everything. All the bullshit disappeared, and it was only the two of them. For a little while, Detroit got to pretend he wasn't broken.

DETROIT LOOKED beautiful and innocent while sleeping. Sometimes, at the oddest of times, it would strike Payne that Detroit had never been a child. The opportunity had been stripped away from Detroit at such a young age. Payne's stomach churned each time his traitorous brain whispered he was no better. He should set Detroit free. Let him be young. Payne was a piece of shit for several reasons. Being with Detroit was just another black mark against his soul. The thing was, not only did Payne love Detroit, he could also recall the first time Detroit had shown at the Den of Payne like it happened yesterday. Detroit's eyes had been dead—like he'd lost all hope. Those eyes, they'd been the only reason Payne had let him stay.

"That's all you want?"

Detroit nodded. "You say that as if it's a small thing."

Payne shook his head. "I'm not belittling your request. Not at all. I'm saying, keep your money, and come here." Payne opened his arms and waited.

Detroit didn't budge. "I need you to take my money."

With a sigh, Payne dropped his arms. "The only way I'll let you pay is if I get one of my guys to do this. They don't know you. It'll be a job like any other to them. If it's me, this is something I would've done at home for free because it's the truth."

The way Detroit blinked rapidly, making Payne worry he might fall apart, kept Payne from calling for one of his employees to take over. "I need it to be a job, but I also need it to be you."

Payne realized this was important, and if Detroit had been a stranger, he would've done as requested for money without question. Detroit deserved the same respect he'd give a stranger—more, in fact.

He gave Detroit a sharp nod and opened his arms again. Detroit looked reluctant and uncomfortable, refusing to meet Payne's stare, but he walked into Payne's open arms. Payne wrapped the man in a tight hug and pressed his lips to Detroit's temple.

"I'm so proud of you."

Payne's throat burned. He blinked, fighting the stinging behind his eyes. How had he not realized before how messed up Detroit was? The guy was always at his house. He practically lived there. Detroit was always smiling. Payne should've noticed the pain behind the gesture.

Detroit's hands landed on Payne's hips. The sound of Detroit's breathing changed. Their hug transformed, becoming... more. Detroit's fingers stroked Payne's sides. Payne's lips moved lower, shifting from Detroit's temple to his cheek. Each breath Payne took felt a little deeper, but less oxygen reached his brain. This wasn't why Detroit had come to him. Payne couldn't step away. He brushed another light kiss across Detroit's cheek. Detroit turned his head. Their lips met.

Payne jumped away. He couldn't meet Detroit's stare. "Sorry. I know... I mean, you didn't... I'm sorry." Fuck. Detroit had come to him because adults had fucked him up, and Payne had immediately tried joining their ranks. Fuck.

"Payne."

Detroit sounded so calm Payne finally met his gaze. He looked beautiful. Aroused. Payne closed the distance between them. Detroit met him halfway.

This kiss was different. Without hesitation. Everything was lost.

Payne shook off the memory. He'd been such an old fool for this man. Detroit slept on with his arm slung over his forehead, oblivious to Payne's inner turmoil. Payne stared at the angry red and jagged scars lining Detroit's arm. He fought the urge to touch them. The need to feel the places where Detroit's life had almost slipped away ate at Payne's mind. No one would ever understand how what he'd nearly lost had almost cost him his sanity.

"I don't want to be your client." Detroit's words had Payne's gaze snapping to his face. His eyes were still closed.

"You're not. I thought you were sleeping."

"I think I was for a minute, but my thoughts are too busy. Micah set me up with a therapist," Detroit said, keeping his eyes closed. "At first, I felt stupid talking to a stranger, but my sessions have made me realize some things about myself." His eyes finally opened. Detroit focused on him with his gorgeous blue gaze. "They've made me realize some things about us." Payne's chest tightened. He was scared as hell Detroit had figured out Payne was no better than every other person who'd tried ruining Detroit's life. "When you told me you never wanted to see me again, I thought my parents were right about me. That I was sick in the head with twisted desires, and I was just getting what I deserved."

"Your parents should be shot."

"I know they're terrible people but knowing that doesn't remove their voices from my head. It's hard to unlearn everything you've been taught your whole life. But I have to start somewhere, and I think it needs to be here. I can't be your client or plaything. If I have any chance of putting myself back together, I can't be those things anymore. My heart isn't strong like some peoples are."

Payne tucked Detroit's hair behind his ear just to give himself a reason to touch him. "You were never a client or a plaything. There's also nothing weak about you. You're right about one thing though. Starting over needs to start here with me apologizing. I shouldn't have kept you a secret. At first, I didn't say anything because you'd come to me with something very personal. Then, I kept quiet about us because of Micah. But, mostly, I didn't tell anyone about us because I was ashamed of falling in love with someone who deserves a normal relationship with someone their age. I can't be younger or normal, no matter how hard I try."

Detroit didn't respond right away. He simply

stared at Payne, wearing a shocked expression. "You fell in love with me?"

"Why are you surprised? I think you've always known that. You've also known why I couldn't claim you as mine."

Detroit sat up and scrubbed his fingers through his hair. He stared at the wall in silence. Payne held his breath. He didn't know what he'd hoped to accomplish by telling Detroit he loved him. Payne only knew he couldn't go the rest of his life knowing he'd never voiced his feelings.

Payne ran his fingers down Detroit's hard back. Even if Detroit was angry or upset, Payne couldn't stop stealing every touch.

Detroit drew an audible breath. "I'm not okay."

Payne's chest tightened at the confession. Unfortunately, Detroit wasn't finished. "And, I think, I never will be as long as I'm with you." Payne's heart was breaking. Detroit still hadn't looked his way. He wanted to see Detroit's eyes, but Detroit didn't accommodate him. "There was a time I would've given anything to hear you say you love me. I would've fallen at your feet. Time has given me some perspective." He turned and met Payne's gaze. Payne stopped breathing at the rage in Detroit's stare. "I deserved to be publicly claimed. If you really loved me, you would've talked to Micah. You know he would've forgiven us faster if we'd been honest. But for whatever reason, you chose to keep me hidden. You didn't want people to know about me. I deserve more."

"You're right. I have no excuse." Payne sat up, wondering if he should go home. He was doing more harm than good. "I think I liked the idea of having something special just for me. Maybe I'm just too twisted to be who you need."

Detroit sprang. Payne found himself on his back and staring into the man's enraged features. "Or maybe," Detroit spat. "You're too big of a coward to love me."

As much as Payne chafed at being called a coward, he refused to lose control. He also recognized Detroit was owed this. "I love you." Payne said the words clear, ensuring there could be no doubt they were true.

Detroit went nose to nose with Payne. "Then prove it with something other than your body. Until you can do that, stay away." Detroit's voice turned pleading on the last word. He sounded broken. "Otherwise, I'm not sure I'll survive you a second time. I'm scared as hell of feeling like your client again. I can't do it."

Detroit's words were like gasoline on the fire. Payne flipped and rolled, tucking Detroit beneath him. His control slipped. "For the last goddamn time, you've never been a client. You're different. I'm different when I'm with you. Hell would freeze before I let a client disobey me the way I let you do as you please. I don't want to control you. I just want to *be* with you. Why can't you see that? Why can't you feel it? No one sees this side of me. You're the only one who knows why I do what I do. Hell, you're the only one who's ever bothered to ask. Please, just please fucking stop." Payne took a breath. His armor forged of discipline fell back into place. Calm settled in his chest. He could do this. He could do anything for Detroit. "If you need me to prove myself, I will. You'll see."

Detroit dipped his chin in a short nod. "Okay. I trust you."

Payne hoped that was true. He would probably test that before it was over, but Detroit needed to learn he was stronger than he thought, and no one taught lessons like Payne.

SEVEN

DETROIT CAME AWAKE WITH A START. HIS GAZE shot around the room. The bed was empty. He knew without getting up to check, the room would be too. Detroit closed his eyes. Even while trying desperately to keep his mind blank, the hurt crept in. He'd woken up alone after a night with Payne countless times. Nothing had changed. That was the first thought that sneaked in. Once that was past his barrier, every horrible thought imaginable came crashing in as well. Payne had said he'd prove himself. Well, he had. He'd proven once and for all he didn't really love Detroit. No amount of pain on Detroit's part would change a damn thing.

He rolled. Paper crunched beneath him. Detroit

dug it out. It was a note from Payne. That wasn't a first either. He had dozens of goodbye letters in a shoebox at his storage unit in California. Leaving was Payne's second biggest specialty.

Detroit,

I had this room booked for a week, thinking I would hang around until I wore you down, and you chose to keep me out of pure annoyance. Now, I think I'll go home. While you slept, I stared at you and plotted the next fifty years. Then the sun rose, and I realized I didn't want to spend the next week in Vegas. This isn't our home.

I know you need me to prove myself. There's only one real way I can do that, and I can't do it here. As much as I'd like to believe you won't wake up angry with me, I know better. Me leaving always pisses you off, and I know it wouldn't matter if I said goodbye or not. Either way, you won't understand. So, I chose to stare at you for as long as possible instead. You're so goddamn beautiful. Why can't you understand that you deserve flowers, poetry, and someone kinky? Instead you always settle for me. I need you to know I'm choosing you over everything too. Like I said, I can't do that from here, because I don't have sweet words or anything, really. All I can give you is a stable life and me, such as I am. Give me a few days and you'll see.

I love you. Don't wake up hating me. We'll be together soon. — Payne

Payne would get his wish. Detroit didn't hate him. He hated himself for giving Payne another morning to leave him. Detroit rolled from the bed and found his clothes. Payne claimed he couldn't prove himself here. Well, he sure as shit couldn't prove himself from hundreds of miles away. The only thing Payne had assured with this move was that Detroit got it—he wasn't important. Payne would never fight for him. They'd never be a real couple.

Half-dressed and with shoes in hand, Detroit walked away. He rode the elevator up to his room, avoiding the stares of people he passed. Anger settled into his chest for the first time. It felt good. He should've gotten mad sooner. This morning was different from the rest. Today, he knew he'd tried. He'd been open and vulnerable, giving Payne a real shot at being together. Detroit hadn't failed. Payne had.

As his room came into view, Detroit spotted Omen leaning against his door. Omen straightened when he caught sight of Detroit. "Oh ho," he said with a laugh. "I recognize that walk of shame. The only thing missing is the broken heels and smeared makeup. Was it a glorious night?"

Detroit barely stopped himself from growling. "How long have you been standing here?" he asked instead of snapping like a wounded dog.

"Not long. I thought you'd like to see the news first thing in the morning." He held up a paper. "Top story on half a dozen gossip websites. There we are," he said, tapping the picture. "Dancing very intimately, according to the article. Here." He passed it Detroit's way. "One of my band mates printed you a copy."

Detroit held out Payne's note. "I have a paper too. Let's trade."

Omen scanned the letter while Detroit unlocked the door. "Wow."

"That's not exactly the word I would've chosen."

Detroit tossed his boots aside. Once Omen followed him inside, Detroit closed the door behind him.

"Sounds like he plans to come back for you."

Detroit shook his head. He couldn't look at Omen. "Well, it felt like he simply left me *again* while I slept."

Omen set the letter aside. "Whatever happens, in the meantime, you have me. My show is right around the corner. I say, you let me spoil you in the world's most therapeutic shopping trip."

Despite his intentions to turn Omen down, his spirits still lifted. Omen made it hard to be unhappy. "I can't let you spend money on me, but I'll be more than happy to watch you spend money on yourself."

Omen waved off his words. "That's tiresome. I already own everything. Plus, I'm not really giving you a choice here. So, grab a shower and let's go. Admit it. You need me right now."

With a loud sigh he didn't mean, Detroit headed for the bathroom. Omen was right. Detroit needed him. Otherwise, god only knew what he might do. Chase after Payne, most likely.

AS PAYNE WAITED for someone to answer the door at Micah's, he marveled at the life his son now lived. The house he shared with his husband was beyond massive and gorgeous. As far as Payne could tell, having endless money hadn't changed Micah at all. His son was happier than ever, but that had nothing to do with material possessions. That was all

Wyld. He'd also quit college, which didn't thrill Payne, but he knew Micah would be fine.

The door swung open. Cortland stood on the other side, holding a tiny brown puppy. It looked exactly like a stuffed teddy bear.

Payne motioned toward the dog. "Oh, wow. Where did this guy come from?"

As usual, Cortland showed no emotion. "Wyld bought him for Micah for Christmas."

"He's adorable."

"He's an asshole."

Payne bit back a laugh at Cortland's deadpanned response. "Is my son around?"

Cortland stepped back. "Theater room. Cut through the living room. It's the third door on the left."

"Thanks," Payne said as he passed, going in search of Micah. He counted doors after cutting through the living room. The door to the theater room was open, but the room was dark. Payne hoped like hell he wasn't about to walk into an uncomfortable situation. After all, he hadn't called ahead. His steps slowed as he reached the doorway. He peeked around the corner. A movie played on the screen, but there was no sound, and no one was watching. Wyld was flipped upside down in his chair with feet on the headrest and his head hanging off the chair. Micah sat on the floor in front of him. They were kissing.

Payne bit the inside of his cheek, fighting a smile. They were adorable. He leaned his shoulder against the door frame and stared at the pair. They were so in love. It was beautiful. Payne hated to interrupt them.

"I love you." Even though Wyld said the words quietly, Payne didn't miss them. He rubbed his chest. Detroit felt a million miles away.

"I love you too."

"Your dad is staring at us."

Payne couldn't hide his smile any longer. "I would've announced myself if things got heated."

Wyld flipped around. "If Micah wasn't your son, I'd call you a liar."

Micah turned and flashed him a smile. "Hey, Dad. Why are you back from Vegas already?"

"Hey, sweetie. Maybe I missed my one and only son too much to stay away."

Micah rolled his eyes, but he still looked pleased. "Wyld is right. You're a liar." Micah's expression turned worried. "Is Detroit okay?"

Payne rushed to reassure him. "He's fine. I had some things to take care of here." He moved deeper into the room and claimed a seat. "Plus, I wanted to talk to you."

"You could've done that over the phone."

"In person is better," Payne assured him. "It's important to me," he explained.

Micah looked even more worried than before. "Okay."

Payne didn't make him suffer. "I needed to see your face, so I could read your expression when I ask, are you certain you're one hundred percent okay with me being with Detroit?"

A huge grin appeared on Micah's face. "Does this mean you're back together?"

Payne didn't hold back. "I think it's more serious than that."

Wyld massaged Micah's shoulders, showing his support. Micah looked ecstatic. "Seriously? I would love that. If you're together and happy, I won't have to worry about either of you anymore. You'll be settled." Payne chuckled. Micah was the adult in their relationship. "Does that mean Detroit is back in town?"

Payne's smile fell. "I'm still working on that

part." It was possible he'd fucked up by leaving without saying goodbye.

"It'll happen. He loves you."

Even though Payne smiled, he didn't have Micah's confidence. If Detroit chose Vegas and his career, Payne couldn't blame him. If the shoe was on the other foot, he wouldn't choose him. No one in their right mind would choose him.

DETROIT HAD NEVER GOTTEN to hang out and watch a concert from side stage before. Omen was fucking amazing. He had presence and talent. People kept trying to talk to Detroit. It seemed those gossip sites carried a lot of weight. Everyone thought he was dating Omen no matter how much they denied it. Omen's people tried waiting on Detroit hand and foot, ensuring he was happy. Omen thought it was hilarious. Detroit not as much. He wasn't used to the attention.

Omen was hyped. It was obvious the man rode the same high Detroit did after winning a fight. Several times, Omen turned his way as he sang, looking ecstatic. Detroit couldn't stop smiling. It had been a damn long time since reality had fallen away, leaving him free to simply enjoy life. Omen had done that for him. By the time Omen ran off stage for the final time, Detroit had to force himself to stay still. He wanted to hug Omen for giving his tired brain a vacation.

Despite being a sweaty mess, Omen was gorgeous in his excitement. His eyes shone bright with life. "Did you have fun?"

Detroit's cheeks hurt from smiling. "So much. You looked amazing out there." Detroit sounded every bit as happy as Omen. It was almost as if he'd been the one performing.

Omen's gaze moved over Detroit's face. The rest of the world disappeared. "You're incredibly sexy, you know? I mean, of course I noticed that fact immediately, but this is different. You're looking at me differently."

Detroit shook his head, feeling like he was failing Omen by becoming like everyone else—star-struck. "I just had a great time tonight. You've never really seen this side of me."

Before Detroit had time to guess at Omen's intentions, Omen kissed him. It wasn't a kiss between friends. There was no mistaking it was sexual. Detroit's mind stopped working. Fuck him. It was amazing. He kissed the man back. Omen was the first to pull away. He held Detroit's face between his hands. His gaze never wavered from Detroit's, as if he sought answers. "I'm—"

"You sorry ass motherfucker." The roar came out of nowhere, bringing both their heads whipping toward the angry yell. A young guy, possibly a year or two younger than Detroit stood, heaving chest and wild eyed.

"I'm sorry, Omen. Someone recognized Keegan from a past show and let him in." Detroit recognized the apologetic man at Keegan's back as one of the guys who'd been trying to keep him happy all night, but Detroit couldn't stop staring at Keegan. He was a wild beauty. Quite a bit of his skin was covered in tattoos and there were two piercings in his bottom lip. His dark hair looked a sexy mess, making Detroit wonder if it was intentional. He didn't know how to react.

"I should go," Detroit heard himself say.

Omen didn't respond. Detroit risked looking away from Keegan to check his reaction. Omen looked torn between anger and devastation. It was a place Detroit understood well.

Omen's gaze never wavered from Keegan. He took a step in the man's direction. "Kee—"

Keegan turned and walked away.

"Go after him," Detroit urged, giving Omen a small push in the other man's direction.

Omen focused on him once more. "I have to."

Detroit flashed him an understanding smile. "I know."

"My car will take you—"

"Go before he gets away. I know how to get back to the hotel."

With a sharp nod, Omen was gone. Detroit didn't watch him go. Instead, he dragged his feet as he made his way outside. He didn't want to risk running into the couple. That wouldn't help Omen's case with Keegan. Instead, he pulled out his phone and used one of the apps to hire a car. With that out of the way, Detroit found himself pulling Payne's number up, and staring at his name. Fuck it. He'd never had any pride with Payne.

Detroit: *Omen kissed me.*

To his surprise, Payne texted him back immediately.

Payne: *I'm not surprised.*

A smile tugged at the corners of his mouth.

Detroit: *I am.*

Payne: *Why? Not only are you the sexiest man alive, you know who you are and you're not ashamed. For someone like Omen, who I've never heard a single whisper of being with a man, you would represent everything he craved in life. Like I said, it would shock me if he didn't try.*

Detroit shook his head and tried not to smile. Payne always knew everything. It was maddening and irresistible.

Detroit: *I didn't realize you knew who Omen is. You didn't let on.*

Payne: *Why would I care? I came for you. He's no one to me. Just remember you are everything to me and I love you. Be careful.*

Detroit: *Always.*

Even Detroit didn't know which part he meant—being careful or remembering he was everything to Payne. Maybe he'd stop being Payne's fool someday. One day, Payne wouldn't be the first person he always texted. Maybe.

"Did he even tell you about me?"

Detroit clutched his chest and spun toward the voice coming from the darkness behind him.

Keegan separated from the shadows of the side of the building. "Let me guess," he said before Detroit could recover enough from his surprise to respond. "He didn't."

Detroit blinked, trying to decide how to respond.

"I'm sorry." Honest to God, Detroit didn't know what else to say.

Keegan chewed his bottom lip, looking way too young while Detroit felt eighty. "Don't be," he said, sounding exhausted. "I got what I deserved for showing up here tonight. It's not on you that I'm so goddamn stupid I keep coming back for more punishment. When I saw that picture of you two, I was just too goddamn mad to stay away. I had to see you in person."

"Okay," Detroit said, feeling lost and like the worst of scum.

"What do you have that I don't? Is it because you're not obviously gay while I am?"

Confusion landed on Detroit like a truck. "What?" The comment had Detroit shaking off his shock and really looking at Keegan. He was beautiful —like supermodel hot. The guy put most women to shame because his makeup wasn't subtle, yet he was so over the top stunning that Detroit hadn't noticed the rainbow eyeshadow around his eyes. Keegan was amazing. But that didn't make sense. "Wait. Omen said he got dolled up for shows and shoots all the time and it wasn't a big deal until he met you."

Keegan nodded. "Then he cared. He cared that I like to be pretty. It mattered that I rarely leave the house looking normal. He loved those things about me in private, but since he'd always believed he was straight until he met me, he didn't like that I confused him. I really think he hated me a little for how I made him feel. Now, he's on the cover of magazines with you. A man. Why? Obviously, you're gorgeous, but why?"

"I don't know." Except Detroit couldn't decide what he meant. He didn't have the answers Keegan sought, but he didn't have the answers to his questions either. Omen had claimed he was the one who wore makeup. He'd said he was the one who knew himself. It seemed to him, things were the opposite. "Can I ask you something?"

Keegan nodded. "Sure. Why not?"

"Which of you broke things off?"

"Me. I realized he would never love me. This hurts more than I thought it would."

The truth dawned, draining Detroit. He lived in a world of liars. Payne was the only person who was ever honest. "I called a car. Would you like to share it with me?"

Keegan shook his head. "It's nothing personal. I know Omen is free to be with whoever, but..." he shrugged, as if incapable of finishing.

"Come on," Detroit cajoled. "I'm not leaving you

out here. Omen and I aren't together. I came to Vegas, trying to forget the man I love, and it didn't work. Omen and I are just friends."

"That kiss says otherwise."

A smile pulled at the corners of Detroit's mouth at Keegan's snarky tone. "I promise you, even if you hadn't shown up when you did, it still would've just been a kiss."

"Mr. Amherst?"

Detroit turned at the sound of his name. His car had arrived. "Just a second." He focused on Keegan once more. "Come on. Let me give you a ride. I'll let you call me a bastard and tell me all about how you'll have a voodoo doll made in my name."

Keegan sniffed, looking on the edge of falling apart. "I don't even know your name."

Detroit held out his hand. "Detroit."

Keegan lightly shook his fingertips as if he loathed touching Detroit. "Keegan."

"Let's go, Keegan. This badly lit parking lot is no place for such a beautiful man."

A hint of a smile crossed Keegan's features. "Just so you know, I'm not helpless or weak."

Detroit kept his face as serious as possible. "The thought never crossed my mind."

With a sharp nod, Keegan let Detroit lead him

toward the car. Detroit set his palm on the small of Keegan's back. Keegan didn't pull away. Inside, Detroit fumed. He would see Keegan to safety, and then he would find out why the fuck Omen had lied to him.

THE IDEA of Omen's lips on Detroit's body had Payne ready to commit murder. His skin felt too tight. He'd picked a hell of a time to retire. There was no outlet for his rage. Payne headed for the basement, needing release. He'd turned his basement into a home gym several years back. In his profession, he needed to stay in shape, but he didn't have much free time. Until Detroit came home, this would be the only release he'd get. Payne stretched and tried keeping his mind blank. He peeled off his shirt and jumped, snagging the pull-up bar. Two sets in, time slipped away.

Payne's mouth watered as he watched Detroit, shirtless and muscles glistening with sweat. His sexy blue gaze never wavered even as he pulled his weight upward over and over again. They watched each other. There was so much hunger between them, Payne couldn't understand how they hadn't burned down the house much less kept Micah fooled. Payne needed to get up. Do something. His dick was too hard. There was no hiding his erection

"This is pointless," Micah said, sounding bored as he set aside some weights. "Even if I wanted, I'll never look like you," he added, waving a finger in Detroit's direction.

Detroit winked. "You're compact—like a tiny runner, and you're beautiful. Don't compare yourself to me."

Fuck. Not only did Detroit not sound winded, he was praising Payne's son. Everything about the man was sexy and under Payne's skin. He couldn't take this torment much longer. Payne tore his gaze away from Detroit and focused on Micah. "Why don't you grab some cash from my wallet and pick us up some dinner if you're bored? Take my truck."

Micah brightened. "Sounds great. You two can finish achieving what I never could, and I'll get..."

"Chinese," Payne supplied with raised eyebrows in Detroit's direction. The closest Chinese restaurant was a twenty-minute drive one way. They'd have nearly an hour alone. It wasn't much, but, damn, Payne needed Detroit.

Detroit dropped from the bar and nodded. "Chinese works for me. You know what I like."

"Me too," Payne added.

Micah headed for the stairs. "I'm on it. See you in a bit."

Payne held still, letting his hunger grow as he listened to the alarm chirp, signaling Micah's departure. Still, he waited, making sure Micah hadn't forgotten anything. His cock jerked with need. His heart ached to hold Detroit.

"Come here." Even Payne heard the unadulterated lust in his tone.

A flush that had nothing to do with exertion touched Detroit's cheeks as he crossed the room. "What can I do for you?" Detroit asked, playing coy.

"You can kiss me and make this ache in my chest go away."

"In that case," Detroit said, closing the distance between them and straddling Payne's lap. His arms encircled Payne's neck. He moved slow. Payne's patience snapped. He lifted up and claimed Detroit's mouth. Relief surged through him the second their lips met. Payne wanted to make love to Detroit, but those needs were secondary to the cravings of his heart. He was completely fucked. Payne knew he was in love with Detroit. No matter how he looked at things, there didn't seem to be any hope for them. It was an outcome he wasn't sure he could endure.

Payne dropped from the pull-up bar and moved to the weight bench. He sat where they'd made love that night. Detroit didn't feel closer. Payne was scared shitless Detroit would never come home to him.

EIGHT

DETROIT PACED. PEACE WAS GONE. HE TRIED counting. Detroit even tried holding the ridiculous vibrating stuffed animal the therapist had given him to calm him. Nothing worked. He'd memorized Payne's parting letter. Every word. He had to focus on something else. Detroit texted Omen, desperate to aim his fury somewhere.

Detroit: *Why did you lie to me?*

Thirty seconds after Detroit hit send, the phone rang in his hand, startling him enough he almost dropped his phone. Seeing Omen's name, he answered. "Hello?"

"Hey," Omen said, sounding every bit as unsure as he should. "Will you give me a second to explain before you tell me you hate me and to lose your number?"

Detroit rolled his eyes. "I just asked you why. Do I strike you as the type to demand an explanation and then rip you to shreds before hearing it?"

"No, but I didn't want to take any chances. I'm guessing after one look at Keegan you've guessed the truth. Beautiful, isn't he?"

"Stunning," Detroit answered honestly. "You're obviously a liar and a fool."

"I didn't set out to lie," Omen said, sounding despondent. "I just didn't expect you to be so brutally real and honest with me. You didn't hesitate baring your soul and showing your every insecurity. The more of yourself you gave, the more I realized I wasn't worth knowing. You've seen real pain. All I've done is dish it out. I'm not worthy of knowing you."

Detroit was torn. He'd thought they were friends. Damn, Detroit was just so fucked in the head, he didn't know how to handle this. All he knew was how he felt. "Whatever happened between Keegan and you, that has nothing to do with me. You saved me from taking that shot alone and then stayed with me while I drank again for the first time. That shit mattered to me." For the first time, Detroit truly understood what Micah must feel like, being his friend. Micah had once told Detroit he'd kept his mouth shut about a great many things Detroit did when it came to relationships. Detroit didn't know if he had the same resolve. Keegan seemed amazing. Omen had too. Damn. He didn't know what to do. Detroit heard himself admitting as much. "Honest to god, I don't know how to handle all this. My coping has never been great. Payne is my strong half."

"I disagree. You're the bravest person I've ever met. Payne is damn lucky to have you."

Detroit took a deep breath. As good as it felt to hear Omen say those words, Detroit wouldn't ever stop kicking himself if he didn't speak up now. "After you ran off last night, Keegan found me. If he isn't the bravest fucking person you've ever met, you haven't been paying attention. Do you have any clue how hard it is for him to be true to himself? He's living in a hate-filled world, giving him the side eye and telling him he doesn't belong. That world includes you—the person who stole his heart then stomped on it. You can tell me it's not my business, but you made it my business when you let people think we're together when you'd always treated him like a secret. You were wrong, and only a real friend would tell you that." Detroit held his breath. Omen would either love him or hate him for being honest.

"So, you're saying we're still friends?"

Something between a snort and a sigh escaped Detroit. "Is that all you got from what I said?"

"No, but I'm dealing with what's in front of me. What do you say? Do I get another chance?"

Detroit stared out his hotel window and smiled like an idiot. "I'm all about the second chance."

Omen blew out a sigh. It sounded loud across the phone. "Thank you. I know you don't believe me, but I don't have many real friends, and next to no one who truly knows me."

Detroit's mind drifted to Payne the way it always did. Payne was that person for him. Everyone deserved at least one human in their corner, especially at their worst. Even as he made small talk with Omen, Detroit's thoughts never drifted far from Payne. He wanted to be where his heart was. By the time Detroit tucked his phone in his back pocket, he couldn't think about anything else. How many times had Detroit considered doing the same thing Keegan had done after Payne dumped him? Showing up unannounced, demanding Payne see the mess he'd made. Hundreds. Thousands. Every single day, at least twenty times a day since Payne destroyed him.

Of course, if he turned up in Payne's space, screaming and ranting, it wouldn't be jealousy driven. It would be desperation. The more time Detroit spent in Vegas, the more the place chafed. If he was still in Cali, he could at least see Micah. They could talk about nothing. Maybe go to dinner.

When someone knocked on Detroit's door, he nearly ran to answer. Even if it was housekeeping, any distraction would do. He could only blink at the sight of Zander.

"You've got fifteen messages at the front desk. All death threats." Zander said the words so dryly, Detroit wasn't sure if he should take them seriously.

"What?" Detroit dragged out the word, thinking Zander had to be joking.

Zander wasn't finished. "I've also received three very generous offers to buy out your contract and set you up for life if you'll agree to let Payne come out of retirement."

Detroit shook his head. "What? Wait. Payne retired?"

For a moment, Zander eyed him, as if trying to decide if Detroit's confusion was genuine. Obviously deciding it was, he dropped the news. "It seems Payne has decided to continue running the day-to-day operations of the Den of Payne but retire from the playroom, so he can focus his energy on you."

Horror overcame him. "No. Payne can't retire.

He needs..." Detroit realized he'd almost said too much. "I'm sorry, Zander. I have to take care of this."

"Of course," Zander said. He didn't look upset. "That's why I delivered the message personally. Some things are more important than money. You need to take some time from the fights."

Detroit liked Zander. While most people only saw the mob boss, Detroit saw there was so much more to the man. "Um." Detroit cleared his throat, feeling uncomfortable. "I've been meaning to apologize. For everything," he clarified.

Zander's mouth lifted in one corner. His light blue eyes screamed understanding. "There was a time when I was green with envy for every person's obituary I read. You're not weak. There's nothing to apologize for. Sometimes, the monsters in our heads are so much worse than any campfire story. Not everyone will understand, but I do."

Detroit nodded, seeing the truth in Zander's eyes. He'd never wish his pain on anyone, but it was nice not to be alone. "Thank you for that."

With a dip of his chin, Zander turned away. He turned back before making it two steps. "Oh, by the way. I know you wanted to fight here because you wanted to start over. Should you decide you'd rather be back home, I'll continue to sponsor you there. I'm not picky."

Detroit's throat swelled. Zander really was a good man. "I'll keep that in mind."

He watched Zander as he made his way down the hall toward the elevator while he tried to decide what he should do. Detroit couldn't handle this over the phone. He would have to go home. Maybe he should've never left.

DETROIT STARED out the window and watched the clouds pass by as the plane cut a path through them. He still couldn't wrap his mind around Payne retiring. Without a release for his temper, Payne might do anything. Everyone was apparently threatening Detroit because they only saw what the sessions with Payne did for them. Detroit was terrified of what not having those sessions would do to Payne. Detroit was the only person who understood. He was the only person Payne had to confide his secrets.

As the son of an abusive father, Payne had countless issues and a temper that rightfully scared him. Between his feelings of helplessness at home and being relentlessly bullied at school, at fourteen Payne had snapped. He'd left another teenage boy hospitalized and barely clinging to life. It had been a horrific mistake and a blessing because juvie had been better than home. The anger management the court forced him into had taught him things about himself. He liked to make people hurt, but he wasn't his father, and he wasn't a bully. In fact, it scared the shit out of Payne that he might one day become either.

Then he'd grown up and met Micah's mother, Kayla. They had an immediate connection—like they'd been born to be best friends. She'd been the first person Payne confessed his twisted thoughts to. When she'd joked he should make a career of hurting people, the idea had stuck. Now, it was what kept him level. He'd never raised a hand to his son. Of course, Micah was such an angel, it had never been an issue. Micah had grown into the gentlest soul alive. Seeing Micah now made Payne feel like he'd beaten his past.

Now, Payne had given up the very thing that had saved him. For Detroit. Detroit couldn't let it happen. He couldn't be the reason Payne snapped again one day. Payne had been aptly named. He needed to dole out the punishment. His sanity demanded it. People like Detroit needed people like him. Maybe there were those who thought they were both a screwed up mess, and maybe they were, but Payne and Detroit fucking needed each other.

Between the flight and the cab ride to pick up his car, Detroit thought he'd come up with something to say.

By the time he reached the Den of Payne and set eyes on Payne, every word dried up inside his mind. Payne didn't notice him right away. His head was bent over his desk as he went over some paperwork. Detroit stared, transfixed. Neither time nor distance lessened Payne in Detroit's eyes. If anything, the man grew larger. He eclipsed all others.

Payne's chin lifted. Their gazes met. Payne leaned back in his chair. Detroit's breath caught. He fought the urge to cross the room and climb into the man's lap. Why couldn't he stop loving this man who always left him?

"How do you get more beautiful every time I see you?"

There it was—the reason he couldn't quit Payne. "Since I'm getting death threats because of you, this might be the last time you see me."

Payne blinked. "Death threats?"

Detroit sighed. He wanted to be angry, but the

emotion he craved wouldn't come. "It seems your clients aren't happy with me right now."

"I have no clients anymore."

"Exactly. How could you do it, Payne? People need you."

Payne's mouth lifted in one corner in the sweetest smile Detroit had ever seen Payne wear. "What about what I need?"

Detroit had a damn hard time holding onto his aggravation in Payne's presence. He wanted to kiss him. More than that, he wanted Payne to hold him and tell him all the things Detroit would never believe on his own. Only when those praises left Payne's sexy lips did Detroit think for a moment anything good could be true of him.

"Tell me what you need." Detroit would give him anything. Fuck. He was an idiot.

HE'D KNOWN Detroit would come. Detroit was the one person in the world who never let him down. If it was the last thing he ever did, Payne wouldn't let Detroit down either. Payne stood. He circled the desk and grabbed two cases. He knew Detroit would recognize them as the ones holding his gear. Detroit's eyebrows rose, but he didn't ask.

"Come on. Let's go." He headed for the door, expecting Detroit would follow.

Detroit didn't budge. "I'm trying to talk to you."

Payne glanced over his shoulder. "There's an empty playroom down the hall. You can talk to me there."

Detroit still didn't follow.

Payne sighed. "You said you trust me, right?"

"Of course." Detroit sounded so damn sure, it punched Payne in the chest.

"Then, let's go."

With a shake of his head, Detroit followed him down the hall. Payne found an empty room and shut them inside.

"What are you doing, Payne?" Detroit asked, sounding tired as Payne pulled off his shirt and tossed it aside.

"You said you trust me. Well, I need you to know I trust you too." He secured a set of cuffs around one wrist and raised his arms toward the hook hanging from the ceiling. "It's your turn to have control. I can answer your questions while you work."

Detroit looked lost.

Payne rearranged his features, showing his fear. "Have you decided you don't want me?"

Detroit scrubbed his hands through his hair the way he always did when he was frustrated. He focused on Payne, looking resigned. "You know I'll always want you."

With a sharp nod, Payne rattled the cuffs at him. "I promise I'll answer any question you may have once you play along."

With a resigned sigh, Detroit peeled off his light jacket and tossed it toward Payne's discarded shirt. Payne's stomach muscles tightened as Detroit moved his way. He was so in love with this gorgeous man. The thought of Detroit taking control scared him a little, but that was the point. Payne's breathing turning shallow as Detroit cuffed his free wrist and helped weave the chain over the hook. Payne could go up on the tips of his toes and fight his way off the hook, but he wouldn't. Detroit would keep him safe.

"Why are you doing this?" Detroit asked, simply refusing to accept his dominant role.

"The blindfold," Payne said, continuing to disobey to see how far Detroit would let him go.

With an eye roll, Detroit moved over to the cases and popped them open. While on one knee and inspecting the goods, Detroit tugged off his shirt.

The muscles in his back flexed. Payne went hard. Detroit needed to blind him. Otherwise, Payne wouldn't last long. The sight of Detroit was too beautiful.

Detroit straightened and crossed the room, holding the blindfold. Payne dutifully lowered his head so Detroit could slide the silky piece into place. He couldn't see a thing. He fought down his panic. It was Detroit. He was safe.

"Why, Payne?"

"Why what?"

Something cold and hard clamped down on his nipple. Payne sucked in a hiss.

"Why, Payne?"

It seemed Detroit wouldn't take anymore bullshit from him. "You told me to prove my love. I'm trying."

Silence met his claim. It dragged on for so long Payne started to worry. Then, he heard Detroit take a deep breath. When Detroit spoke, his voice was deeper. Payne could picture the flush on his cheeks. He would know Detroit's turned on voice anywhere. "Tell me the safe word."

"Lemon." He wouldn't be using it. Detroit had no idea how much punishment he could take. He listened as Detroit crossed the room again and rifled through the cases. Payne held his breath when footsteps moved his way. Cold metal touched his stomach. He jumped at the unexpected move. Detroit circled his body, dragging the clawed item along his skin as he went. Payne swallowed. His tongue felt too big for his mouth. He couldn't speak. All he could do was feel. Detroit walked a full circle around him, stopping where he started. The claws disappeared only to end up in the center of his chest. Detroit ran them down his torso, stopping at Payne's waistband. Each breath Payne took came out in a pant. The claws didn't hurt, but they'd definitely leave a mark. Payne's cock jerked and leaked. He was turned on to the point of pain.

Metal hit the floor, making Payne jump. Detroit's warm hands landed on his hips before tracing the waistband of his jeans. He stopped at the button.

"Please," Payne begged. It was out of his control.

"Please, what?"

Payne swallowed. He'd never expected to be this close to crumbling this soon. "Please, Sir."

Detroit worked the button loose and slid Payne's zipper down. "I'm going to strip off your clothes. You will stand here, proud in your nudity. Is that understood?"

"Yes, Sir."

Detroit removed the remainder of Payne's clothes while touching him as much as possible, but never where Payne wanted it the most. Detroit left him again to dig through the case. When he returned, something slick and soft brushed his erection. Payne had to lock his knees to stay upright. He should've known Detroit wouldn't hurt him. Instead, Detroit had chosen to torture him with pleasure without release. The material stroked him again too softly to do more than fuel his insanity.

"You said you'd answer anything. I expect compliance."

"Yes, Sir," Payne choked out through his rapidly drying throat.

"Why did you retire? I want the truth."

"To bring you home."

Detroit rewarded him with a firmer stroke of silk up his length. His cock jumped in response.

"You left me."

"I came home." At Payne's defiant response. The silk disappeared, and a solid smack landed across his upper thigh. He knew immediately it was a crop since the sting was minimal. "Try again, Payne."

"You needed me to prove myself. The best way I

can do that is by giving up who I am to show you I'd rather have you than anything, including my sanity."

Detroit moved so close, Payne could feel the heat radiating off his body. His lips pressed against the center of Payne's chest. A stinging began behind Payne's eyes. Being robbed of his sight had him feeling more than he liked.

"I would never ask that of you," Detroit whispered against his skin.

"You didn't. I gave it freely."

The lightest of touches brushed his dick, forcing the air from Payne's lungs. Detroit didn't move away. The clamp on his nipple disappeared. Before blood rushed back to his nipple, Detroit's hot mouth covered it. Payne tilted his chin to the ceiling and sucked air. The light and torturous brushing of his cock didn't relent. Payne feared he'd come from the crushing lust alone.

"What would you do for release?"

"Anything," Payne said, sounding desperate even to his ears.

"Would you forget about retiring?"

Payne's breathing turned ragged. The pressure beating at his crown had him on the edge of sanity. "If it wouldn't cost me you." No matter how badly he needed release, he still wouldn't risk losing Detroit.

The pressure on his cock increased a hair. Goddamn. He hadn't edged like this in years. It was hell. "Then promise me you won't retire yet."

"I swear," Payne said, hearing the desperation in his voice. But he couldn't be the only one making promises. "Swear to me I won't lose you."

Detroit licked his nipple again before responding. "Exactly how far would you go to keep me?"

"Damn, baby," Payne breathed, finding it harder by the second to be submissive. "There's nothing I wouldn't do. Nothing."

"Would you marry me?"

Payne's mind stuttered to a stop. He'd sworn to never marry. Detroit knew that. He didn't want to trap anyone with his insanity. But Detroit wasn't scared. No matter how twisted or dark Payne went, Detroit merely begged for more. They were the perfect match with Detroit's need to hurt and Payne's cravings to cause harm. Anyone else would think he was psychotic. Detroit always drank it in, flourishing under Payne's care.

Detroit took a step back, stealing his touch away. His voice turned hard, but Payne heard the hurt lacing his every word.

"I guess when you say there's nothing you

wouldn't do, what you really mean is you wouldn't do anything."

"Lemon."

Detroit took a ragged sounding breath. "That's what I thought." Detroit's hand encircled his wrist as he unlocked the cuffs. He didn't remove the blindfold. The moment one wrist was free, and the hook no longer held him, Detroit moved away.

Payne ripped off the mask. Detroit was headed for the door. With the cuffs still hanging from one wrist, Payne went after him, overcoming Detroit before he reached the door. With a tug, he spun Detroit around. The instant their gazes collided Payne fell to his knees. "Please? Let me be a normal husband to you in the eyes of the world while you keep me sane at home." Even though he knew Detroit had only suggested marriage to test how far Payne would go for him, now that the idea was in his head, Payne wanted it. He needed Detroit tied to him forever. They belonged together. No one else understood them the way they got each other.

Detroit's hardened expression never wavered. "No. You don't want that, and I can't live with knowing you don't want it." He visibly swallowed. "Just take back your clients and have a good life."

Payne flew to his feet and shoved Detroit against

the closed door before he could get away. He couldn't pretend to be docile any longer. His brain itched under the pressure. "Do I look like you're twisting my arm?"

Wide eyed and unblinking, Detroit shook his head.

"You are fucking marrying me. I'm not asking. You belong to me. Is that understood?"

"Yes, Sir?"

"Repeat it back to me, Detroit."

"I belong to you."

Payne's rage wasn't assuaged. "Like you fucking mean it, Detroit. Like you understand you won't ever be touching anyone else again."

Detroit's features softened. "Baby, even if you never wanted to get married, I wouldn't touch anyone else."

Payne went flush against Detroit, loving the way their bodies felt when their chests met. When their heartbeats tried kissing. "Why won't you be touching anyone else?"

"Because I belong to you," Detroit dutifully repeated. This time Detroit sounded firm and happy —like he believed the words leaving his lips.

Payne's lust returned full force. "You left a job unfinished. Drop your pants."

A flush immediately appeared on Detroit's cheeks at Payne's hard tone. Payne leaned away barely enough to give Detroit room to comply. The backs of his knuckles brushed Payne's erection as he unbuttoned his jeans. Payne's gaze never wavered from Detroit's as he stripped.

As Detroit pushed his jeans down his hips, Payne finally moved away, turning his back on Detroit. He headed for the open cases. "I want all your clothes gone by the time I turn around." Payne didn't require a response. He knew Detroit would comply. After unlocking the final cuff and tossing it aside, Payne found a tube of lube he'd kept stashed in his case just for his sessions with Detroit. No one else shared his body. Only Detroit brought him release. No one else was allowed to see him vulnerable.

He coated his cock with lube as he headed back to Detroit. Detroit stood nude and waiting. "Face the wall. Palms flattened against it."

Detroit's gaze slid down Payne's body. His gaze heated as he slowly complied to Payne's command.

Payne's mouth watered as he watched Detroit's hard muscles flex throughout his body as he assumed the position demanded of him. He stroked Detroit's back. "Ass out, Detroit." Detroit shuffled backward. His spine curved as he bent over while still braced against the wall. Payne massaged the globes of Detroit's ass. His cock jumped as if trying to get closer. He spread Detroit's cheeks. His gaze never wavered from his task as he toyed with Detroit's asshole. "I expect to hear your pleasure. If you like what I'm doing, I want your words. Understood?"

"Yes, Sir." As a reward for complying, Payne curled two fingers inside Detroit and massaged. A deep moan escaped Detroit. "I love you."

Payne froze at Detroit's confession. He'd admitted to loving Detroit. It hadn't occurred to him that Detroit hadn't said the words to him before in that tone—like he still felt that love all the way to his soul. Detroit's claim stole the oxygen from the room. For a moment, Payne could only stare at Detroit in frozen silence. His body reacted without his brain. The tip of his cock prodded Detroit's asshole, slipping inside an inch. As the tight heat squeezed him and tried sucking him deeper, Payne's tongue unglued.

"I love you too." A cry bounced from the walls as Payne impaled Detroit. Payne brushed his hands down Detroit's back, soothing him even as he pumped inside him. "You're such a good boy. I'm so proud of you." Detroit panted as Payne praised him.

"You make me wish I never had to do anything else. Stroke yourself, beautiful. Feel what I do."

Detroit immediately shifted positions, bracing himself with one hand while jacking off with the other. "Goddamn," he whispered, sounding ready to blow.

Payne smacked his ass hard. "Slow down. You're not allowed to come yet."

A low moan escaped Detroit.

Payne changed angles, ensuring he hit that sweet spot with each thrust. His vision narrowed to a pinpoint.

"Damn, Payne. You're perfect inside me. I love it when your huge cock fills me, stretching me, and claiming me. You're making me crazy. I need to come. Please?"

Payne couldn't focus on anything but the building pleasure. He reached, needing that explosion. "Do it," Payne demanded. Detroit's hole clamped down on Payne's dick a half second before his greedy ass sucked Payne's cock, milking him into ecstasy. Payne swore he saw stars. Waves washed over him as his cock jerked inside Detroit's ass. He gasped for air and stroked every place he could reach. Words left his lips. Promises he meant even as he knew he'd never remember them. The impact of the day slammed into him. Detroit had forced him to swear he wouldn't retire. Payne had demanded Detroit marry him. Everything was about to change in his life. Detroit would be with him every day. They'd go to sleep and wake up in each other's arms. Happiness choked him.

Payne spun Detroit and hauled him against his chest. He held tight, needing to know the man was real. There truly was someone out there for him. Someone who accepted him as is. It was like after years and years, all his prayers had finally been answered. The power of his miracle made it hard for him to breathe.

"I'll keep you safe. You'll never regret me," Payne swore.

"I never have, baby," Detroit said, stroking him and soothing him. "Through everything. No matter what. I've always believed you are my other half."

Goddamn. He loved this man. Nothing else mattered as long as they were together. They would be whole.

NINE

WITH HIS EYES CLOSED, DETROIT SAVORED THE sensation of Payne placing light kisses on the shell of his ear. There was no place better than being cuddled up in Payne's lap in their favorite recliner with blankets weighing them down. Even though it never got too cold in Santa Clara, the nights were chilly. Payne wasn't making it easy to watch the movie.

"Children, please? You're being very distracting over there," Micah fussed. He didn't look their way, but Detroit could tell he was smiling by the curve of his cheek.

Detroit snuggled deeper into Payne's arms. "I don't know what you're talking about. We're watching the movie and minding our business."

Payne's hand slipped inside Detroit's underwear, making the final word come out in a squeak.

"Okay, my beautiful angel," Wyld said, coming to his feet. "I think we need to give the newlyweds their space."

Detroit started to protest, letting them know they didn't need to leave. After all, Payne and Micah needed to be spending time together before Micah and Wyld left again in a few months for the summer. Payne's fingers encircled his cock, freezing the words in his throat.

Micah set his bowl of popcorn on the coffee table. "Okay. It does seem like we've overstayed our welcome."

Payne groaned and released Detroit. "No, baby. You're always welcome."

Micah flashed them a smile. "I know. That was my way of trying to pass the blame because I want to go home and act stupid with my husband."

A bark of laughter escaped Detroit. "We're not the only newlyweds here."

"It's true," Wyld said, coaxing Micah to his feet. "Plus, we've become homebodies. We like our space."

Yeah. Detroit knew. The pair did nothing but love on each other at home. He was certain they didn't like leaving that comfort. Detroit's phone buzzed, pulling his attention away. He checked the face of the device. Seeing Keegan's name, he opened the message.

Keegan: *This party sucks. Being single sucks.*

Detroit: *I know, babe. Stay strong.*

"Should I be worried about you texting with Keegan?" Payne asked against his shoulder.

Even though it was ridiculous, Detroit smiled. He kind of liked this new jealous side of Payne. "You know better. No one can compete with you."

"Oooh, I want to meet this Keegan," Micah said, cutting in.

"Much love and we can show ourselves out," Wyld said, helping Micah into his jacket, and steering him toward the door before he could hold them up any longer.

"If you insist," Payne said, snuggling with Detroit like the pair had already left.

The moment they were alone, Detroit turned his head and kissed the spot beneath Payne's ear. "Mhmm, my sexy husband."

"I think that's me," Payne said with a laugh.

"We've run off our guests. What should we do now?"

"This," Payne answered, wrapping Detroit

tighter in his grasp. "We haven't gotten enough of this. At least, I haven't."

Detroit closed his eyes and savored the moment. He'd never expected to have any of this, especially with Payne. Detroit still couldn't believe Micah had accepted them. More than that, Micah seemed thrilled to have Detroit as part of the family.

A stuttered breath escaped Detroit. "I've never been so scared of losing anything." Sometimes panic attacks still sneaked in when he least expected it. Therapy helped, but Detroit worried he'd always be at least a little bit of a mess.

Payne made a shushing sound against his neck. "You're okay. I'll keep you safe. Take a breath."

Detroit sucked in a deep breath.

"Good boy. Let it out."

Detroit released his breath.

"Do it again."

Detroit did as commanded. The sudden shaking of his insides ebbed. Payne knew exactly how to care for him when Detroit's mind betrayed him.

"I love you, baby. You can't lose me. No matter what, we'll always find our way back to each other— like two halves of the same soul. Tell me you believe in us as much as I do."

"You know I do."

Payne bit his earlobe. "That's not what I said. Tell me."

Detroit's heart rate increased. "I believe in us."

"That's better." At Payne's praise, Detroit closed his eyes and relaxed into Payne's hold. Every worry, real or imagined, fell away in Payne's arms. He knew they'd always find their way. They'd never stop reaching for each other no matter how life tried pulling them apart. Detroit felt like he'd won the lottery in Payne. For as long as he lived, he'd ensure Payne felt the same with him.

KEEP an eye out for the next book in the series, Sugar Bastard.

PLEASE CONSIDER LEAVING a review at the retailer where this book was purchased. Reviews really help with a book's visibility, which ensures I can continue writing. Thank you, Charity.

ABOUT THE AUTHOR

Charity Parkerson is an award winning and multi-published author with several companies. Born with no filter from her brain to her mouth, she decided to take this odd quirk and insert it in her characters.

*Seven-time Readers' Favorite Award Winner
  *2015 Passionate Plume Award Finalist
  *2013 Reviewers' Choice Award Winner
  *2012 ARRA Finalist for Favorite Paranormal Romance
  *Five-time winner of The Mistress of the Darkpath

Connect with her online:

--Join my street team: facebook.com/TeamCharityParkerson
  --Sign up for my newsletter: http://bit.ly/CharityNews
  --Website: charityparkerson.com

--Facebook: facebook.com/authorCharityParkerson

facebook.com/TheMenofSin

--Twitter: twitter.com/CharityParkerso